HIT AND RUN

By Jason Moore

Dedication

I would like to dedicate this book to Justin Moore, Cyndi Moore, Jonathan Moore, Earl Moore, Kristin Robertson, and Irma Thompson. Thanks for the love and support in helping me with "Hit and Run".

About myself

I live in a small town in Virginia. When I'm not writing, I enjoy reading, traveling, hiking, hunting, and spending time with family and friends. I am truly blessed I get to do what I love. I give glory to God for everything good in my life. Without Him, nothing is possible.

Chapter 1

"What do you mean, you hit a deer!" Lindsey yelled at Robert as he tried to explain why there was a used 2007 Honda Pilot, instead of the usual four-door Accord, parked outside their apartment. "There aren't any deer on the interstate." She went on looking from him to the car, then back again.

"I called you earlier today and told you I was going into the country to look at some real estate for a buddy of mine." He argued back, knowing full well that wasn't the truth.

"No, you didn't." She grabbed her cell phone from her jean pocket. "In fact," she browsed through the call log of her phone, "you haven't bothered to call me all day."

"Well, I know I told you," he started, "maybe at breakfast or when I was getting ready for work." He walked past her toward the front of the apartment. He didn't want her to know he had been in the country remodeling real estate for them, instead of looking for one for his friend.

The one-bedroom palace they called home was too crowded in the small housing complex. The walls were too thin and the neighbor's whispers sounded like a megaphone enunciating every word. It was all he could afford after spending most of his savings on their wedding just over a year ago.

Robert Armes worked at a local real estate company, which didn't pay much. With the economy in bad shape, he was lucky to *show* a house, let alone expect someone to *buy one*.

It was pure luck when he came upon the estate in the country one night after driving off following yet another fight between him and Lindsey. His high beams gleamed off the FOR SALE sign that was partially covered by some overgrown brush. For the past month, he had been sneaking around, talking with the small company just east of the surrounding county that owned the property. They were going out of business, and Robert was able to get a good deal before the agency went completely under. The town he'd called home since birth was starting to die off. Everyone was moving to the city in search for jobs that were becoming scarcer with each passing day. He knew he had to get the house just right before springing it upon his now-red-faced wife who was currently following him into the living room. He tossed his jacket on the couch.

"Sometimes, I think what I say goes in one pretty little ear and out the other." Robert turned around to smile at Lindsey as he pushed back a stray hair.

"Don't you dare try to sweet talk me," she batted his hand away, "and pick up your coat." She nodded toward the strewn jacket. "I worked all day trying to get this house in order. I even cooked a nice supper for you to come home too." She marched over to the kitchen.

"I made your favorite—Chicken Alfredo, tossed salad, and garlic bread." She motioned to the neatly decorated place setting on the flea-market table with cardboard underneath that kept it from wobbling. She leaned over and blew out the candle, the smoke dancing up to the ceiling as she made her way toward the bedroom.

"Enjoy your supper," she called over her shoulder as she slammed the door behind her.

Robert could just picture the neighbors rolling their eyes as yet another dramatic episode of Robert and Lindsey had just aired.

He pulled a chair from the old table, sat down—fork in hand—and started to eat without really tasting the food.

How long has this been going on, he wondered while silence emitted from the back of the room. Nothing but the crunch of the lettuce in his mouth could be heard, as if even the neighbors too were afraid to make a sound.

He had known Lindsey for twenty months, eight months of dating and twelve months of marriage. Seven of which were pure happiness followed by five months of misery. Something had to change in order for them to move forward with their lives together. He was working as hard as he could to earn anything that he could. How could it be his fault no one wanted to buy a house and move into an area that was decreasing in value? Whatever the reason, she would find a way to blame him—he was always wrong and she was always right.

Why did I get married so young? Everyone said it wouldn't last. We rushed into marriage without thinking it through. He started wrestling his fork with the Alfredo.

He could just hear his friends saying, "I told you so." "What was I thinking?" he grumbled, stabbing at the noodles. Love and money eventually run out, and for some reason, it seems to happen around the same time. "I need to fix this." He got up from the table and made his way toward the master bedroom.

"Come on, honey," he coaxed to a closed door. "I'm sorry about the car, but the insurance people said we were covered. And we have this *new* used car until then. Heck, it's nicer than the junk we've been driving around in the first place. It's going to be OK." He gently cracked open the door. "Come on, can't we just talk about this?"

"I don't know how much longer I can do this," she muffled into her pillow.

"Do what?"

"This. *Us.*" She got up from the bed.

He could see she had been crying.

"It's always one thing after another—the car, me not able to find a job, money, and how we never have any. That dinner in the other room. I didn't make that. Earlier today, my sister came by with it in an oversized basket. Amy told me she'd made too much for her church gathering and this was left over. She was lying. I could see it in her eyes, but I couldn't bring myself to question her."

"Come here." He tried to pull her in.

"No!" she protested, "this is all just...I had to lie about cooking dinner tonight because I was too ashamed to tell you that my sister brought it. How can we live like this? If I can't confide in you about the little things, how in the hell are we supposed to talk about bigger problems? Because that is all this is—one big problem."

"Come on now, that's not true." He looked into her sorrowful eyes, seeing the pain he'd caused her. "We always get through our problems together."

"We never get through our problems," she glared at him. "We put it off, push it aside, or wait until one of us snaps."

"If we didn't resolve our issues, how could we be where we are today? We have a year's marriage behind us. We couldn't have done that without overcoming little conflicts."

"Where we are today?" She stared at him with disbelief. "A year behind us? What—our marriage is something of a goal to meet? If we make it to the next day, we can just call it a victory? No, Robert, this isn't how it's supposed to be."

"How is it supposed to be, Lindsey?"

"That's not something you can ask and be given an answer to, Robert, and then just hope it gets better."

"What do you want me to do?"

"I want you to care, to care about me, about us, about where we're going."

"I do care," he said defiantly, getting up to hold her in his arms.

"Yeah right." She pulled away from his grasp.

"Just leave, go," she said, now completely turned away from him. "Maybe we need a break from each other, just go."

"I'm not leaving like this." He stood tall.

"You don't get to stay this time, just go." Tears were rolling down her face. "Just get some air."

"Are you going to be here when I get back?" He turned toward the door.

"I...I don't know, maybe, just give me some air. Can you do that for me?"

"Are you going to be here when I get back?" He asked louder, more determined.

"Just give me some air!" She pushed him out the door, closing it behind him.

He went through the living room, picking up his jacket as he went, wishing that fixing his marriage could be as easy as putting his jacket in the right place when he came home.

"How could she do this?" he wondered as he crossed the doorway, leaving his apartment. He had honestly tried to make her fall more in love with him. Surprise visits home from work just to say he loved her. Cheap flowers from the dollar store to make her feel like he understood her better. Yet nothing worked. She seemed to get angrier with every futile attempt. She'd complain he was spending money they didn't have, even if it was for her.

As he turned the key in the lock of his rented Honda Pilot—the cause of tonight's disturbance—he turned back around to face his life. He breathed softly in the afternoon air as the sun was starting to set over the horizon. He hopped into the car, started the ignition, and sped off—not once looking in his rearview mirror as he turned the corner.

Robert traveled the familiar back roads of the countryside. In twenty minutes, he would be at the spot where he could fix all of his problems. A place, if given the right love and care, would turn everything around for him. The drive took him past winding roads, deeper into the country.

He pulled into the graveled driveway passing the now SOLD sign completely hidden by the brush.

He slowly continued up the driveway. The house wasn't far off the road, but far enough the passing traffic, as little as it may be, wouldn't disturb the new occupants.

Robert parked the car, switched the engine off, and sat there as the car hissed while the engine cooled down. He stared out the window just to take in the scenery, not really looking at anything in particular.

The grass was overgrown in front of the house and traveled around the side. Weeds were crawling up the front porch over aged steps, the middle one broken from the past inhabitants. The white paint was starting to peel off the old wood from years of weather damage and poor upkeep. Nobody had lived here for years.

On the deck were two rocking chairs, a gift from the owner, along with a few other items. Robert thought it was just an easier way to get rid of them, but he didn't complain—he didn't have much, and anything would do. The two rocking chairs were a matching set. One was ruined from being on the edge of the porch where rain could drip off the side of the house and run down the chair, taking the paint along with it. The other was in perfect condition. Nobody would buy only one rocking chair from a matching set. The only people who bought and used wooden rocking chairs made to be outside were married elderly people so they could sit and watch their grandchildren play in the yard.

Robert hoped to have children running around the yard, playing baseball on a Sunday afternoon while he and Lindsey sat holding hands and rocking in perfect rhythm together. They would watch their kids and their innocence run around the yard. A dream that seemed to slip further and further from reality each day.

Robert got out of the car and shuffled his feet up the driveway to the porch, making sure to skip the middle broken step as he went. He was growing more and more accustomed to this house, especially since he visited every time he and Lindsey fought—which happened more often lately.

The crickets were softly beginning their nighttime song in the background, a sound not often heard back home. He turned around and rested on the railing to stare out at the darkening sky, listening to the chorus of the cricket's ballad.

It was so peaceful—quiet, but not too quiet, with enough space to breath and still not feel completely isolated from the world. The perfect place of refuge to run to when things became heated at home. However, if things didn't get better between him and Lindsey after he told her about this investment—where would he run then?

He hated lying to her about what he was doing, but he believed it would work out better if he could surprise her with this place. He had managed to get enough money for a down payment by taking out a small loan and saving little bits from each paycheck. The small amount was used to finance this house, which seemed like the right decision at the time. Now it seemed like a black hole taking his marriage along with all the money he had to his name.

The sun had disappeared, leaving the moon and stars to take its place. The crickets carried on their song, growing softer in the night air.

Robert crossed over the porch, pushed back the screen, and made his way inside.

The house smelt of dust and abandonment as he entered the empty hallway. The rooms were dark, the electricity and water disconnected while renovations were being made.

The house was a two-story country home with genuine wood floors. The man that sold him the place gave him a brief history of its past, emphasizing how it was built nearly eighty years ago by hand, as if that made a difference. The seller was trying to talk up the place so he could get a higher premium for it. Then it was taken by the bank when the previous owner went bankrupt. That's when the house was bought by the realtor company who hoped to flip it and make a fortune.

The front door opened to a hallway, which led to the living room breaking off to the left. A kitchen was on the right, with two rooms, along with a small guest room, a full bathroom, and what used to be a formal dining room were on the bottom floor. Upstairs gave way to the master bedroom, along with a full bath and two more bedrooms.

Robert felt his way to the stairwell, each step echoing throughout the house, reassuring Robert that he was truly alone out here. He had grown accustomed to the familiarities of the residence. And with the moonlight outside streaming through the smudged windows, he had just enough light to get upstairs.

After making his way to the top of the staircase, he felt around for the wall to lead him in the right direction. He slowly walked down the hallway and into the only room he had come here for.

On the floor in the middle of the area was a battery powered lantern, hammers, and some nails. Across the room, against the finished part of the wall, lay sheetrock.

He fingered the surface of the battery-powered lantern until he found the power switch that barely lit up the room. After moving it closer to the wall, he went back for the hammer and a handful of nails. He started hammering into the night, fixing up what would later be the master bedroom. He knew if he could fix this one room, he could fix anything, and then everything would just fall into place. This one room was the key to his happiness.

Any chance Robert could, as well as any time he and Lindsey fought, he would drive out here and work on this one room. He would tear down the old walls and put up newer ones, the best and only way he knew how.

"This'll work," he mumbled to himself in between hammer strikes. "This has to work," he repeated. "There's nothing else to do, nothing else to try."

Robert continued to beat out his frustration on the white sheetrock as the time slowly passed.

Outside, an owl hooted softly into the night. The wind brushed against the trees as the nightlife of the grounds came alive with its usual activity. The only other sounds heard were the clamoring of metal hitting metal as nails were being driven into wall.

Robert yelped as the hammer and nail clamored to the floor. "Son of a—" he yelled to the empty room as he shook his thumb, already starting to swell from where the hammer smashed it. "Ugh," he continued moaning as he walked around, hopping to ease the soreness, kicking over the lantern with his sudden movements.

"Mother—" he yelled, more in anger than pain at his own clumsiness. "Why am I even trying?" he questioned himself. "What's the point?"

He didn't even bother turning the lantern off or putting the hammer and nails neatly back in the center of the floor for his next visit. Each one more frequent than the last.

He fumbled out of the room, staggered down the stairs, out the house and down the porch steps, forgetting to skip over the broken one. He face-planted into the gravel, adding more bruises to his misery.

He lay in the gravel for a few minutes, his hands starting to bleed where he cushioned his fall, his thumb throbbing with even more pain than before. He covered his face in the ground, hiding from the already darkened night, hiding from the world.

"Why is this happening to me?" he grumbled, pushing himself up onto his feet, wiping his hands on his pants leg, blood smearing on them. *Just another thing Lindsey is going to be asking about when she washes clothes.*

He walked towards the rental. She wouldn't worry if he was OK, or what happened. Just more work for her to do to get the stain out so he couldn't spend money on a much needed newer pair.

"I don't even care anymore!" he screamed at the night sky as he opened the unlocked car. "I don't even care anymore," he repeated, defeated at his attempts to repair the old house.

He climbed into the vehicle, turned the key in the ignition, and whipped out of the driveway, only to see a faint glow in the upstairs window reflecting in his rearview mirror. The lantern was struggling to shine through the dirty glass but would soon lose the fight and eventually go out—just like his marriage.

Robert headed back toward the apartment the same way he normally did when he left the countryside home. He traveled down 95 South—it was quicker—although he wasn't quite sure why he was in such a hurry to get back. There was nothing there but bitter anger waiting to pounce on him when he walked through the door. Over the past few months, it always turned out that way—there was an initial fight where he would leave the house for a certain amount of time. Then when he came home, they would start back up again until one of them either got tired out or gave up. Finally, they would fall asleep, usually with him on the couch.

He glanced at the digital clock in the car, which burned a dull 7:30 orange. He wondered if that was enough time for her to cool off. He looked out the window to see a Chrysler Sebring zoom past him.

He could see the two kids laughing from the glow of the dashboard inside their car, almost hearing the laughter as they went on down the road. He wished he could make Lindsey laugh like that again.

The exit to the small apartment complex was coming up, but Robert didn't get over into the right lane. He couldn't bring himself to go home just yet.

The bleeding had stopped and the pain in his thumb started to fade, but it would be nothing to the headache waiting for him when he did return.

The off-ramp was half a mile away, but he still didn't get over. The exit came and went, and he felt a little more relieved as it did so. The next exit came and went as he continued to drive farther and farther down the interstate, going nowhere specific.

Thirty minutes passed, then an hour, as he continued driving down the road, the traffic was starting to die off as busy commuters were returning home after a long day of work.

Robert drove in silence until he saw a familiar sign up ahead, one that had left his mind a while ago. He pulled off the interstate onto the highway that he had only traveled once. One that was only full of happy memories from when he and his buddies had come here about a year ago. He had been much more carefree and happier with the world then.

He passed a couple of streetlights as he scanned the area. About two miles down the road, he found what he was looking for. He pulled into the parking lot that was starting to fill up with the nightlife of the small town. He hopped out of the car, forming a grin on his face, because this was the one place he had never brought Lindsey to and she had never seen. There was no memory of her here.

He walked toward the door and could already hear the laughter coming from inside. He strolled in, determined to have a good time, or at least have a cold beer and remember what it was like to just have fun with his friends. The night they stopped here to refuel, the night before his wedding.

The bar was dimly lit—TV's were mounted to the wall and every sport imaginable was playing on the many screens that circled the top of the ceiling. Chatter was coming from every direction and Robert felt more at home here than he did with Lindsey. He pulled up a stool and waited for the bartender to come by.

"What'll it be, fella?" the brunette girl asked behind the counter, ready to take his order.

"Whatever is the cheapest," Robert answered waiting for the beer to be placed in front of him. Robert took one big swig of the drink and instantly felt better. He sat on the stool and began to drink, oblivious to the redhead on the other end.

Chapter 2

About his third beer in, and several handfuls of peanuts later, Robert started to feel a little better about himself. The more he drank, the more he forgot about his troubles. He turned around on the bar stool to take in the scene before him.

Everyone was having a good time. The place was almost full. Over in the corner, some sort of party was going on. It looked like a bachelor's party taking place. He wanted to go over there and warn the new groom, but he let it pass as he took another swallow of his beer.

The music was playing through the speakers as the waitresses hustled around the room, filling orders and taking empty drinks from the tables and refilling them with new ones, bigger ones.

He watched a guy try to sweet talk some woman into giving him her number with some cheesy pickup line he'd heard from a movie. No luck came to the man as he brushed off the rejection and went a couple of tables down the room to try his magic on some other unfortunate lady.

Robert laughed to himself. "Poor soul."

"Excuse me," a woman's voice sounded a couple of seats down.

"What?" Robert said in confusion as he turned around.

"Were you talking to me?" she said, a little agitated

"No, no," Robert stuttered, taken back.

"Then who were you talking about?" she inquired. "Everyone here is having a good ole time. So who could be the poor soul you are referring too?" She stopped for an answer but quickly continued, not giving Robert time to respond. "Just because I'm here alone, drowning my sorrows at the bottom of a cup after a huge business deal just went south. One that would have given me a manager's promotion along with a pretty good pay raise and full dental and doctor's insurance, that doesn't mean I should be pitied. Especially by you." She finished what was left of her drink in one big gulp as she hit the counter with her other hand, beckoning the bartender for one more.

Robert stared at her in disbelief as the brunette refreshed her drink. The bartender looked at her with questionable eyes, trying to decide whether or not she should cut her off.

"Last one, Rebecca," was all she said.

"Oh, shut it," she pushed back.

"I wasn't talking about you," Robert said

"Yeah, yeah," she mumbled

"No, really, I was talking about that young man over there using lines to pick up women at a bar. It's cliché, really."

"Well at least he's trying," she said between sips.

"I know, I just meant…" but he trailed off, not sure what he meant himself.

"You come here often…Rebecca, is it?" he watched her closely.

"No," she defended herself rather harshly. "You got a name?" she asked, completely changing the subject as she picked herself up and moved one bar stool closer to him, leaving only one empty seat between them.

"Robert," he heard himself say without thinking.

"And what are you doing here on a Wednesday night, Robert?"

"I don't think that's really any of your business. What are you here for?"

"I just told you in my little outburst. That's just like all men. Don't listen unless it has something to do with them."

"Hey," Robert said a little offended

"Hey, nothing. What are you doing at a bar, alone on a Wednesday night, especially if you're married?"

"How in the world do you know I'm married?"

"Maybe you're gay."

"What are you talking about?"

"The ring on your finger." She nodded to his ring. "Gay, or married?"

"Married."

"You don't sound too happy about that."

"I was married, now I'm divorced," he lied. "Should I celebrate?"

"Some people do," she said, now moving over to the empty bar stool between them, closing the gap.

"What do you do for a living?" she asked, continuing her interrogation.

"I'm a doctor," he continued lying.

"Well, I'll be. A doctor."

"Kind of the family business." He was running out of things to say.

"Ha!" she laughed taking another sip of her drink.

"What's so funny?"

"I just don't think families should work in the same field as each other. Let me guess, the same hospital?"

"No," he said, trying not to agree with her.

"Oh, well still," she continued, "I bet that makes for some interesting conversation around the holidays. Discussing who made the most money and who helped the most patients." She laughed at her own joke.

"What do you do?" he mimicked her question.

"I'm a real estate agent," she replied, then took a swallow of her drink.

"Really?"

"Yeah, yeah, I know, real glamorous, but I'm good. I just wasn't today." She took another sip of her drink.

"Where do you work?" he asked. "Anywhere around here?"

"Ha!" she laughed. "A few states over."

"Then why in the world are you here?"

"The people we are doing business with have been clients for years. They wanted to set up a branch on this side of town. I had to fly out here and check everything for them. The market, the building, the location, everything. I have been here for about a month now, and today they said no. A big waste of my time and efforts. I get to fly back out tomorrow evening, thank goodness."

"Sorry to hear about that." Robert didn't know what else to say.

"You don't have anything to be sorry for, it was those idiots I work for." She was now almost completely done with her drink.

"So what happened in the divorce?" she switched the subject back to Robert.

"Just different interests and we grew apart."

"So why are you still wearing the ring?"

"I guess I've just grown accustomed to having something there," he replied, twisting the ring around his finger.

"You're kind of cute," she said playfully, dancing her skinny fingers up his arm.

Robert took her in full gaze, really noticing her for the first time. She was small but not petite, with red hair that fell straight down her back. Her eyes were soft, hazel, and she had small freckles that covered her nose.

"Umm... thanks. You're not too bad yourself."

He thought she blushed but couldn't tell if it was just the alcohol. Her breath didn't smell as bad as he thought. Maybe she hadn't had as much to drink as he assumed.

"You're too kind." She swallowed the last drop in her cup. "You know," she started to say sheepishly. "I'm only in town for one more night and my hotel isn't too far from here, and you are obviously still trying to get over your marriage. Maybe we can help each other out."

"Excuse me?" He couldn't believe what he was hearing—never had anyone, or any woman, ever come on to him so strongly.

"Come on," she said now, getting up off the stool and pulling at his sleeve.

He put a twenty on the table to cover his drinks just before he let her escort him toward the door.

The last thing on his mind was Lindsey.

Chapter 3

(What would have happened if he had stayed)

"Just leave, go," she said, now completely turned away from him. "Maybe we need a break from each other, just go."

"I'm not leaving like this." He stood tall.

"You don't get to stay this time, just go." Tears were rolling down her face. "Just get some air."

"Are you going to be here when I get back?" He turned toward the door.

"I...I don't know, maybe, just give me some air. Can you do that for me?"

"Are you going to be here when I get back?" He asked louder, more determined.

"Just give me some air!" She pushed him out the door, closing it behind him.

He went through the living room, picking up his jacket as he went, wishing that fixing his marriage could be as easy as putting his jacket in the right place when he came home.

He walked toward the doorway and stopped. Something was pulling at him to tell her the truth about what he was doing, about the house he was trying to surprise her with. Robert contemplated his decision.

He closed the door behind him as he stepped back into the apartment. This time, he went to the coat closet to hang up his jacket before making his way back to the bedroom.

"Lindsey, I have something for you." He tried to sound as sweet as possible.

"Go away!" she shouted from the other side of the door.

"It's a surprise that I think you're going to like," he persisted.

"Go away."

"It's a house," he blurted out, not knowing what to say.

Silence came from the other end.

He waited a few minutes and heard nothing.

"Honey, are you OK?"

Silence

"Honey."

Nothing

"Say something please, anything."

He waited for what felt like hours, then heard quiet shuffling of feet as she stirred in the other room. Then a small click from the once locked door as it opened up slowly.

"You bought a...a..."

"...a house," he finished for her. I wanted to surprise you. I've been working on it for a month now and thought if I had more time I could fix it up a little bit to make it better before I showed you."

"You bought a house?" she repeated, dumbstruck.

"Yeah," he replied, not sure what to make of her reaction.

"You bought a house," she repeated again.

"You're going to have to say something else honey," he grabbed for her hand, breaking her daze.

"You bought a house!" she screamed, more in joy than anger. "And you didn't tell me!"

"I'm telling you now," A small smile appeared on his face.

"Where? When? How?" she asked, excitement glowed in her eyes but nervousness echoed in her voice.

"It's about twenty minutes from here on a small back road that isn't too far from the interstate. It's bigger than this place and has a nice enough yard for some swings and room to run. I already told you when I bought it—about a month ago—and as for the how? I've been taking little bits out of my paycheck each week before I put the rest in the checking account. I also had a little money from my childhood fund I didn't spend on the wedding. I know I should have told you sooner, but I thought I could get it all done."

"It doesn't matter now," she said, pure excitement in her face and voice, "you bought me a house." She started to dance around the room. "Can we go and see it?"

"What, now?"

"Yeah, what's wrong with now? It's still a little light outside, you said it was only twenty minutes away," she said and walked toward the door. "Where are the keys? I want to test out our new car."

What had happened to the girl that was so mad at him minutes ago? he wondered as he once again went to get his jacket, this time from the coat closet.

27

"You even hung up your jacket!" she exclaimed as she reached for hers too.

"Well, the hundredth time's the charm," he said as she started to laugh.

"Come on, let's go." She sounded like a little kid who was getting ready to go to a toy store with the promise of one gift of her choosing. "I can't believe you bought me a house." He could hear her already jumping to get into the car as he turned around to lock the apartment door behind him.

The smallest thing makes the biggest difference, he thought as he hopped into the passenger side, a big smile on his wife's face as he told her which way to go.

Robert's phone was vibrating from his pants pocket, which lay strewn on the hotel floor as he awoke from his sleep. He jumped out of bed, forgetting there was someone else lying right next to him.

"What's going on?" She stirred in the sheets, stretching.

"Nothing," he answered her as he reached his phone to hit the silent button. Lindsey had called.

"Who's calling you at one thirty in the morning, another woman perhaps?" She laughed a little.

"Yeah, my four o'clock wants me to get there a little earlier," he played along as he started to pull on his jeans.

"Ha," she laughed. "Last night was fun. Next time I'm in town, I'll look you up."

"Well...if you told me where you lived, I would return the favor." He scanned for his shirt, spotting it on the desk chair.

"Ohio," she said after a brief pause. "Columbus, Ohio."

"Well, there you go." Robert looked up. Next time I'm in Columbus, Ohio, I'll look you up." He pulled on his socks. "Don't worry about the sale, you'll get a bigger and better one next time. Do you have a number I can call in case I need to buy some realestate in Ohio?" He turned back around to smile at her.

She stopped for a second, then reached around to the bedside table for some paper to write on.

"I was only kidding."

"No you weren't," she said and met his gaze with a half-hearted smile.

"Here you go." She held out the piece of paper for him to take. "Don't I get one too?" She tried to look offended as she nestled back into the sheet.

Robert reached for the same parchment as he scribbled down his cell phone. Lindsey was nagging at him in the back of his mind. What was he doing— trying to save his marriage and start up a relationship at the same time?

"Here you go," he repeated her words as he held out the paper with the seven digits on it.

"Thanks." She rolled over. "Now get out, go meet your four o'clock."

"I'll tell her you said hello," he called over his shoulder as he went for the door. I'll see you later." He left the room, knowing full well he would never see this woman again in his life, but then why had he given her his real phone number? Why didn't he just make one up? Could part of him really want to be with a person he'd just met a few hours ago?

He waited for the elevator to take him down to the lobby. He did the walk of shame in front of the night staff that met him with sideway smiles as he strolled through the automatic doors with a quickened pace.

He climbed back into the Honda Pilot for the long trip home, looking at his phone again before starting the car. His cell had cut off on him. The battery was dead. As the car roared to life, he flipped his phone on the passenger seat, pulled out of the half-filled parking lot, and sped off toward the interstate. This time going the opposite direction from whence he came. The roads were empty on the way back, something he could relate to.

Robert took the exit to get home, the sidewalk streetlights glaring on his windshield as he hurried back. He was replaying earlier events over and over in his head, wishing he could take it back but still glad it had happened. Maybe this was a wakeup call for him. Maybe this was the crossroads in his life—which way should he choose? Should he try to make it work with him and Lindsey, or should he bail out of a sinking ship?

"I don't know what to do!" he yelled out, now only five minutes from the apartment.

What's going on over there? he thought as he noticed lights coming from Jefferson Elementary School. It was after two, too late for anybody to be there. He slowed down to get a better look, not noticing the stop sign as he rolled on by.

Wham!

"What the—" he burst out, while slamming on the brakes, the tires screeching as he did. He peered over the dash, noticing it was suddenly darker than it was a minute ago, even with all the lights from down the street. His right headlight was out and there was a small dent on the hood.

What did I hit? he wondered, peering further out at the seemingly empty road.

Under the lamp about four feet away lay something.

"Oh great, another deer, now Lindsey is really going to kill me," he moaned. "Now this car is ruined. What else is going to go wrong tonight?"

He started to edge the car forward, using his one good light for guidance. He turned the wheel to get a better look at the unfortunate deer that had dared to cross paths with Robert.

"Poor little guy," he whispered. *What is it with my luck and Bambi?*

Now, almost right on top the animal, he rolled down his passenger side window and peered out, looking down. It started to move.

"Oh my..." Robert began, letting the moan of the helpless person laying on the ground finish his sentence. *What have I done?* He stared in fear, paralyzed, unable to move.

31

After a few seconds, the sounds from someone in grave pain brought him back to reality. He had to do something, but what?

He climbed out the car and approached the agonized victim that lay face down on the concrete, arms twisted into an unnatural position. Surely, they were broken. Blood was gushing out of the left leg, poring over onto the streets, forming a rapidly increasing puddle by the second.

" Help!" he screamed out into the night. But the school was too far away to be heard and nobody was around this part of town at night. He didn't know what to do. The morning air nipped at him as his mind raced. His heart threatened to pound out of his chest. He was unsure of what to do next. He didn't want to move the injured person, afraid he may do more harm than good.

"I'll be right back," he said, leaning down to speak. "I'm going to go get some help."

He took off toward the school. He started to scream at the top of his lungs as he ran.

"Anybody out here? Hello?" He continued running as fast as he could, knowing this person's life was in his hands. He was only a few feet from the entrance, a few feet from help before he stopped screaming, stopped running, stopped moving.

What are they going to think? The police would see somebody on the road, seriously injured, possibly life-threatening, and me with a broken headlight on my car. This along with the frontal damage, it wouldn't take a genius to put two and two together. The police would know I did it. His mind was whirling now. *What if this turns into a fatality, then what? Whether I meant to or not, I'm going to jail for negligence, at the very least reckless driving. And with alcohol on my breath, well everything else goes out the window.*

Robert stood there, the school so close he could hear the music coming from behind the doors. He scanned the building, looking for an outside phone. Surely, they had one. This was an old school that wouldn't have gotten rid of payphones, even after the cell phone age had made them obsolete. He spotted one along the front side of the building, next to the vending machine. Running over, he thought about what to say once he dialed the number.

Rolling down his sleeves, careful not to touch the phone with his hands, he pulled out a pen from his pocket, and with his right hand dialed the number.

"Nine-one-one, what's your emergency?" said a voice on the other end of the phone.

"There's a person lying outside of Jefferson Elementary school, corner of 12th and 5th, on the ground, hurt badly. I think there must have been a hit and run, please hurry." He spoke with a deep voice, unlike his own.

"I'm sending help right now," came the dispatcher's reply on the other end of the line. "Can I have your name?"

Robert hung up the phone and jetted across the field toward his car, the one headlight beaming in the darkness. He reached the figure on the ground and quietly said, "Help is on the way."

There was no movement. Blood was continuing to pour from the leg. The moaning had stopped and there was nothing but silence from the street.

Robert jumped in his car, careful not to hit the body, drove two blocks down the street, put the car in park, and shut off his one working light along with the engine.

He waited ten minutes until the emergency squad could get there, hoping that it wasn't too late for whomever was lying on the road. Off in the distant, he could hear the sirens blaring, signaling they were on their way.

A part of him wanted to leave, to get out of there, run as far away as possible, but he waited until he saw the red lights flashing. He would wait until the emergency squad got to the person lying helpless, waiting to be rescued. Robert didn't leave until he was sure the EMT had arrived.

He watched as they rushed to the victim then ran back for a stretcher. It wasn't until they started to load the gurney and got ready for transport that he started the engine again.

By that time, nobody would have noticed a black Honda Pilot, with one working headlight, pull out from its hiding spot to turn the corner, vanishing into the night.

"Honey, is that you?" came a sleepy voice from under the sheets as Robert came sneaking into the room. "What time is it?"

"It's late, go back to sleep," he replied as he began taking off his shoes and socks.

She pulled the covers back slightly, "you smell like cigarettes." She wrinkled her nose as she turned back over.

"Yeah, I went to the bar." He said, taking off his pants and shirt as he climbed into bed.

"Oh great, how many drinks did you have at that bar?" Lindsey questioned. "Why don't we just flush what little money we don't have down the drain? At least that way we could both be spared the smell you bring back home."

"Not again, not tonight, just go back to sleep."

"Yeah."

He began replaying what had happened in the past seven hours in his head. He had managed to screw up his marriage, hit someone with his car, and then run from the scene of the accident all in one night.

"Ugh," he groaned into the pillow. He couldn't stop thinking about that body being loaded onto the stretcher and into the ambulance. *Did the emergency squad get there in time? What if they hadn't?* The vivid memory kept playing over and over, like a broken record.

Would they ever find out it was me? He kept tossing and turning in bed. He hadn't touched the phone, or even made eye contact with the person hit, so there was no way he could be identified. *What about the car?* He tossed some more. Surely, there was broken glass at the crime scene where his headlight got busted but what could be depicted from glass fragments? There was no visible blood on the car, so DNA couldn't be matched with his car to the victim.

"Quit turning," said a disgruntled Lindsey from her half-awakened state.

"Sorry." He tried to lay still. *What am I going to do about the car? Does the rental insurance cover it? I'll have to get there early in the morning before Lindsey gets up.* He kept thinking as soft snores came from the other side of the bed. *Could they fix the damage to the vehicle in a couple hours?*

He hadn't noticed any other major damage to the car when he'd looked it over—just a broken headlight and dents on the front side. No blood. That should be fixed in a few hours.

Maybe they'll just give me another one and just charge more for the insurance. His mind wouldn't sleep. *What am I going to do? I never should have left. I should have just turned myself in.*

Robert lay there, unable to sleep, every event that happened to him that night racing around his brain. He glanced over at the clock—4:00 a.m. That was the last thing he remembered as his mind went blank and the world went dark for about an hour.

Lindsey pulled up in front of the two-story house. Robert could feel the excitement beaming out of her as she stared in awe at the biggest surprise of her life.

"This is our house!" she gasped as she gazed out the window. "When you said house, you really meant house. I was expecting a small one-floor, two-bedroom shindig, but you bought a castle. I can't believe it!" she squealed with anticipation.

All Robert could do was smile.

"So how much was this place? Gosh, it looks like a fortune." *She was unbuckling her seatbelt, ready to jump out as soon as the car stopped moving.*

"It's not as bad as you may think. I was able to get this place cheap. The company who bought this place from the bank was going out of business and I offered a good deal."

The car rolled to a stop.

"The man said it's been on the market for about a year, but the location isn't the greatest for retail value. I just happened upon it one day, called the number, took out a small loan, and added the little money I saved up. In a month's time, it was mine after all the inspections were done."

"You took out a loan? How much of a loan?" She looked to him for an answer, but more questions followed before he could reply. "How long will it take to pay off? How could you do this? We don't have any money as it is."

"I told you, a small loan, under fifty grand, and I've already started paying it off with the money taken out of my paycheck. Plus, the money we've been paying for rent will now go toward the mortgage. We can do this. I wouldn't have done this if I hadn't thought it all the way through. Like I said, it took a month to work out everything, but here we are. Our own home."

He got out of the car. "Come on, you should see the inside. It needs work, but it's pretty amazing."

"All right."

"Be careful." Robert pointed to the broken step. "Like I said, this place needs some work."

"Oh my, well, that can be easily fixed." Her tone was optimistic.

"Now, I have to warn you." Robert stood at the front door. "I've been working on this place off and on, but not as much as I wanted to."

He was lying. He was working on it more than he wanted because of the fights between them.

"This place has huge potential and the owner threw in all the furniture he either didn't want or couldn't give away, so there's a start. Watch your step, this place is a mess. You may accidentally catch your foot on something."

"Just open the door." She was dancing with excitement.

"The electricity doesn't work, and we don't have running water yet. I didn't see the need to pay for extra things until we were living here."

"Just open the door!"

She reached for the screen door.

"Come on now, I want to see the inside."

He could see the anticipation in her eyes.

"Hold on, I need to get the key, I left it in the car," he said as he moved past her.

"Forget this." She pushed the screen door back and turned the knob on her future. "I thought you needed a key?" She looked over her shoulder.

"I thought you wanted to see the inside." He smirked, pushing her in and closing the screen behind them, making sure to leave the door open to let in what little sunlight was left.

"Wow." She stared at the open room. "You weren't kidding about this place, were you?"

"This is the part where I said I told you so," he said as he hugged her from behind, "but it has potential. You have to see the bigger picture." He let go of her and made his way into the empty space.

The room to the left was empty but for a small chair leaning up against a wall. The floors were wooden but in good shape, with normal wear and tear that usually comes with an old house. The place smelt of dust and abandonment, and it was obvious that nobody had lived here for a very long time. The ceiling was white and covered with cobwebs from corner to corner, attached by floor-to-ceiling wallpaper that covered the entire room with faded pictures of flowers.

"This is where we could have a small couch and table to meet guests when they come in, sort of like a formal living room, but smaller." Robert started waving his arms at where the furniture would go. "And this wallpaper, we can easily tear down and repaint it. I bet it's begging to come down. We can make this work, like you said outside." He started making his way back toward her. "So...what do you say? Give it a chance because I can't get my money back." He looked into her eyes. He could see tears starting to swell up. "Say something."

"I love it." She met his gaze and leaned in for a kiss. "It's absolutely beautiful. Let's look at other parts of the house."

"I'm so glad you like it." He took her hand and led her toward the stairs. "I want to show you something."

"What is it?"

"I think you're going to really like it."

"I know I will, I already love this house, and I've only seen one room." She followed him down the hall.

"Ta-da," he said as he pushed open a door that was already partially cracked. "This is the master bedroom." He made his way into the room.

Lindsey wiped the tears that were coming back into her eyes.

"What's the matter? I thought you would like it."

"I'm just so happy."

"Come here." Robert pulled her in. "We're going to work on this place together, start building memories and then a family. I think we'll be able to move out of the apartment in about a month, depending on how fast we work on this place. I've already talked to the electrician and the plumbers about the water and electricity. They gave me the go-ahead, so when we're ready, all I have to do is call. Everything is up to code structurally, even though it looks a mess."

"Let's start moving in a week," Lindsey whispered into his shirt.

"A week? We won't have this place ready in a week. We're pushing it for a month's time."

"I'm not working. I'll come out here night and day and clean out a couple of rooms for our things. We don't have much anyways, and we can stay downstairs until we get this room up and running." She eyed the hole in the wall where Robert had been putting up sheet rock. "I don't want to stay in that apartment any longer. Like you said earlier, we'll be saving rent money. Let's start right now." She noticed the hammer and nails in the middle of the room.

"All right," Robert said as he lifted up the sheetrock against the far wall, "we'll be in our new home in a week and out of our crummy apartment. Don't you want to see the rest of the house before you start construction?"

"Nope," she said as she pulled the sheetrock to the wall and hammered away.

She never ceases to amaze me, Robert thought as he held up the board.

They worked on that room long after the sun went down, using the battery-powered lantern to see.

They started rebuilding their new home, marriage, and themselves when that first nail went into the wall.

Chapter 4

"What time is it?" Lindsey asked, rolling over to look at the clock. "Why are you up so early? It's five in the morning. Surely you can't be showing a house this early." She curled up into the blankets to keep the warmth from escaping as Robert got out of bed.

"I have to run an errand," was all he could think of.

"An errand, this early?" she exclaimed staring up at him. "Another lie! Why can't you just be honest with me? What are you doing up so early?"

"A buddy of mine thinks that he might have some work for me to do on the side. You know, to earn some extra money," he paused, "because you can't seem to find a job."

"Oh," was all she said, not having the strength to argue back after last night's round.

"Well here." She moved to get out of bed. "Let me see if I can find you something to eat in the kitchen." She placed her feet on the wood floor and shivered a little bit. She reached for her slippers and robe.

"You don't have to."

"You need to have some strength, in case something does come up." She made her way into the kitchen.

"Thanks," he said quietly, feeling terrible about lying again to his wife, and even worse about last night. He prayed it was all just a vivid dream.

"What do you want?" she called from the kitchen. "Cheese and crackers or bologna and crackers? We don't have any bread or I would make you a bologna and cheese sandwich." She opened up the fridge door. "Oh," she said, looking at the meal from last night. "You can have this leftover Chicken Alfredo, although that's not really breakfast, but if you want, it's yours."

"No, you have it," Robert said from the bedroom. "I'm going to hop in the shower, just surprise me with something when I get out."

"OK."

How can two people act like this? he wondered as he started undressing. *Last night, we were both mad at the world and each other, but today it's like a brand new beginning.* The water was warming up as he looked himself in the mirror. *I just don't understand. Our marriage is bipolar.*

He jumped into the warmth of the shower, trying to rinse every action from last night off him. Maybe if he scrubbed hard enough, everything would just go away down the drain and be lost, out of sight, out of mind.

The warm drops felt good. The water pressure was terrible, but he felt secure behind the soap-scum-covered glass, as if he could stay here forever and just leave everything behind.

If only things were that simple.

Too quickly, the water turned cold and he knew that his seven minutes were up. It would take another hour for a burst of warm water.

He grabbed a tattered towel from the closet and wrapped it around his waist as he stepped from the bathroom back to the bedroom. He rummaged through the drawers to find something decent to wear.

"Breakfast is ready," came a slightly cheerful voice from the kitchen. "You'd better get it while it's room temperature."

"I'll be right there."

He finished tying his shoes and slipped on his twelve-dollar watch.

"What are we having?" he asked, trying to sound optimistic about the rationed feast that was breakfast.

"Well, I heated up some of the Alfredo from last night. I kept some for myself. Then I made an assortment of cheese and crackers, as well as bologna and crackers, but I'm going to need at least twenty dollars to go to the grocery store so we can have something for tonight."

She came over to sit with him.

Robert reached for his wallet, hoping he hadn't spent too much money at the bar. He opened it to find three twenties and a five-dollar bill. "This is all the money I have until I find some work or sell a house," he scooted it across the table, "unless you want to put more money on our credit card. I'm pretty sure we've almost maxed out those."

"I'll be careful with what I buy," she said, picking up the money and putting it in her robe pocket.

"Don't lose it."

"What? Like on a drink? I'm sorry," she said as she lowered her head and then started to pick at some dried food that had stuck to the table.

"Hey," he said softly, "look at me. There is nothing to be sorry about. I shouldn't have left you last night. I'm the one that should be apologizing."

For more things than you know, he thought to himself.

"I made you leave." She looked at him.

"Yeah, but I didn't have to."

"Well, I'm sure if you didn't, then I would have."

She started to cry. She always cried about something.

"Don't," he said, more annoyed than upset. "Let's start over, give each other a clean slate." He reached out for her hands.

"OK," she muffled through soft tears, reaching out.

"We can make this work."

"We sure can," she answered, "now finish your breakfast and go bring home the bacon," she said through a weak smile.

Robert gobbled up what was left on his plate, more in a hurry to get out of the apartment than out of hunger. He grabbed his coat and gave Lindsey a small kiss on the head. "I'll be back shortly."

"OK."

"I love you."

She gazed up at him. He hadn't said those words to her in a long time.

"I love you too." She leaned in for a kiss that was long overdue. "Now get out of here," she remarked playfully.

"I'll see you soon," he said over his shoulder.

Robert went out the door into the dark, chilly morning. It was quiet in the neighborhood, which he was glad for. He walked toward the car, wondering if he should wait until the sun started to rise to drive. He didn't want to draw attention to himself with one headlight.

After debating with himself for a few minutes, he knew he couldn't go back to the apartment without Lindsey getting suspicious and he couldn't just sit here. He hopped in the car and slowly pulled out, carefully, looking for cops at every turn. After getting on the main road for a few minutes, he found an empty parking lot and pulled in under a tree.

The rental place wouldn't be open until seven, and the sun wouldn't be up until six-thirty. He turned out the lights, put the emergency brake on just in case, and pushed his seat back as far as possible.

After getting as comfortable as he could, he leaned back, closed his eyes, and pushed all thoughts to the back of his mind. He fell into a restless dream of the accident.

"It's time to go, it's late." Robert draped his arm over Lindsey's shoulder as they stumbled down the stairs and into the first room they'd seen.*

"I love this house," she said staring up at him.*

"You haven't even seen the whole house, wait till it's light outside." He matched her gaze.*

"I can just feel it, the way I felt on our first date at that cheap diner downtown."

"That was when you knew?" He looked at her bewildered. "If I remember, that night was terrible. I spilt spaghetti down the front of my shirt and knocked my glass of water in your lap. That was the worst date for me."

"Well, you made me laugh when it was all said and done, and I knew you were nervous. You were really trying hard to impress me. That's what did it for me. Nobody ever tried to show they cared for me. Well, not at our high school." She laughed as she kissed him on the shoulder.

"I can't believe that was the night that did it for you."

"Why, when was the night for you? When did you know?"

They walked out onto the porch.

"The night I took you to the county fair, remember?" he started the story, "when we got on the Ferris wheel and it took us all the way to the top. I remember just looking at you and how beautiful you were that night. You were laughing all the way up, not afraid of anything."

Robert and Lindsey were in a tight embrace, leaning on the rail peering up into the night sky.

"I think this might be my new favorite memory," she said as she leaned into his chest.

"Mine too," he whispered, resting his chin on her head.

They were both tired and sweaty after spending hours upstairs putting up new walls. They stopped because the battery in the lantern

48

died and the light went out on them, but that didn't matter. They stared up into the night sky.

"Do you want to sit on the rocker?" he asked. "You can sit on my lap. The other chair isn't too sturdy."

"Sure," she yawned a response.

She fell into his lap and draped her arms around his neck as he started to rock her to sleep, like she was a little girl. He sat there watching her rest as the night sounds of the country sung all around them.

I'm so glad I told her, he thought to himself, pulling her even closer so she wouldn't slip.

His legs were starting to fall asleep, but he kept on rocking—nothing would make him stop.

A couple hours passed as he continued watching her breath in and out slowly, peacefully. He was falling in love with her all over again.

"Wake up," he whispered into her hair, "look over there."

The sun was starting to rise over the horizon.

"Hmmmm." She stretched her arms as she wiped her sleepy eyes. "Wow," she exclaimed, glancing out, putting her arms back around the nape of Robert's neck.

"Our first sun rise at our new home," he whispered in her ear.

"It's beautiful," she whispered back. "Have we been here all night?"

"Sure have." He smiled at her.

"I can't believe it." She moved to get up but fell back, her legs stiff from being in one position for so long.

"Haha," Robert let out. He couldn't help it. He caught her on the way back down. "Nice and easy." He pushed her up.

"I think I got it this time." She smiled as she moved again, this time successfully.

Robert rose with her, just as stiff from sitting for so long. He stumbled too. His legs were still trying to wake up.

"Let's go." She reached for his hand as they made their way back to the car, skipping the broken step as they walked down the porch.

He opened the car door for her, jumped in the other side, and pulled out of the driveway toward the direction of their now-temporary home. Lindsey had already fallen asleep again in the passenger seat.

Chapter 5

"What do we got?" The stern voice of Detective Phil Collins rang out through the police station as he dropped a manila folder onto his desk with a loud thud.

"A hit and run," a young detective answered, turning around toward his boss.

"Where?"

"In front of Jefferson Elementary School at the corner of 12th and 5th streets. The call came in about two thirty this morning," he replied.

"I need to know the specific time," he barked out as he took a swig of coffee from his cup. *These young kids don't know anything about the force. They're getting younger and younger every year, with less experience*, he thought as Jones, the newest addition to the force, fumbled through the case report, looking for the answer.

Collins had been on the force for thirty years, too young to retire and too old for a new job. He didn't mind the work. He enjoyed the chase and the satisfaction of putting bad guys away. It was the inexperienced newbie that got him frustrated. He didn't have time for incompetence and didn't care for negligence.

"Two forty-seven," Jones called out from his desk in a haste to please his superior.

"That's a seventeen minute window you threw away." Collins glared across the desk at the young policeman.

"Sorry sir."

Jones lowered his head.

"Make up for it right now," Collins said as he logged onto his computer. "Where is the victim now?"

"Uhh…" Jones reached for the folder again.

"Come on, son" Collins snarled as he pulled up MapQuest.

Jones was rapidly turning the pages in the folder, "Lakeside Memorial Hospital," he spat out.

Collins typed in the location and took another sip of his coffee. It was the caffeine that kept him going. He wasn't as young as he used to be and he knew it.

"Come on, you stupid machine," he yelled at the computer, which was taking a long time to load.

Jones was standing nervously across the desk, trying not to do anything to upset him.

"Here we go." Collins scanned the screen, memorizing the directions. "It's twenty-five minutes away. Get your stuff and let's go."

Collins, for all his detective skills, couldn't get anywhere without getting lost. He knew the county like the back of his hand, knew where everything was. Take two steps across the county line—it was like a different world to him. He didn't care for unfamiliar territory.

Jones jumped to his desk and grabbed his bag. Collins downed the rest of his cup and went to the door. Jones was right behind him.

****

The sun glared through the window of the Honda. Robert rubbed his eyes, trying to wake up. He glanced at his watch to check the time—seven thirty. He had slept longer than planned. The car rental agency would be opened now, and he needed to get there before they were too busy.

He didn't want anyone to see his broken headlight, afraid any suspicions could lead back to him after the news of last night's events broke out.

Robert started the car, noticing the once-empty parking lot was starting to fill up with early morning workers reluctantly beginning their day with the same boring routine. He backed up and made his way to the road, driving the speed limit and keeping his eyes peeled for any policemen.

The drive was quicker than he thought given the early morning traffic. He pulled into Larry's Rentals, a locally-owned dealership.

Larry was the average car salesman—gut out past his nose, hair slicked with too much grease, and a bowtie that symbolized arrogance neatly arranged with a suit that cost too much. He owned every car place in town. He would take trade-in from customers buying new cars from him, then take the old cars and put them in the rental lot. It was cheaper than trying to sell a used car. If someone liked the rental they were using, they could buy it. Easy and simple, not at all like Larry.

Robert pulled into the visitor parking space and took a deep breath, already starting to sweat. He opened the car door and made his way toward the entrance.

"Just be calm," he whispered to himself, "nobody knows what happened. Just say you hit another deer."

"Can I help you?" a salesman's voice rang out through the showroom.

"Uh, yeah," Robert answered, stalling for the right words.

"I was actually in here yesterday. I rented a car, my old one is being worked on, and well, I was in a small accident."

"What kind of accident?"

"The thing is, I don't know," Robert replied pitifully.

"I see," he looked at him rather suspiciously. "What happened?"

"I was driving along and suddenly hit something. My headlight is messed up along with the right front end of my car. It's not too bad but bad enough to need a quick fix."

"And you don't know what you hit?" The man stared at him in disbelief.

"It was late. I wasn't really looking." Robert shuffled.

"OK, well we're going to need something for the accident report. You did get the rental insurance on this vehicle, right?"

"Yeah."

"OK, well let's go out and see what we have." The salesman made his way toward the door. "By the way, I'm Tim." He turned around and stopped to shake hands.

"Robert."

"OK, Robert, is this your car?" He pointed toward the Honda with the dent. "Yeah."

"It doesn't look too bad. Must not have been driving fast."

"No, I was going through a scho—a scooter park," he finished lamely.

"A scooter park?" The salesman looked puzzled. "Never heard of it."

"You know, that place where kids go to ride their bikes and rollerblade and things with wheels—a scooter park."

Robert walked around the car pretending to check the other headlight.

"A skate park?"

"Yeah, a skate park," Robert reassured him, "that's what I meant. I never know what those darn things are called."

"I know what you mean," Tim started up, "I have a twelve-year-old son and every week it's something different. Maybe next week it'll be a scooter park, who knows." The man started laughing. "Well, like I said, this isn't too bad, should be able to fix it in a couple of days."

"Can I get another car?"

"You can, but the insurance coverage for it will be through the roof. If you decide to get it."

"How much?"

"Five hundred."

"Five hundred?" Robert repeated. "I don't think I'll get the insurance this time."

"Suit yourself," Tim replied as he inspected the damaged end of the car again, "but you may want to from the luck you've been having. Didn't you say you were here yesterday because your car was in the shop?"

"Yeah, but that wasn't my fault."

"And this was." He peeked up at Robert.

"No, this wasn't my fault either, like I said, something just hit me."

"And like I said, you may want to reconsider that insurance. Doesn't matter to me, but we'll still need a copy of your license and insurance for record, in case you are in another accident. But you'll have to pay full price for that one, buddy."

"I'll pass."

"All right." He gave up on trying to get the five hundred bucks from him. "Maybe you'll change your mind."

"In the next fifteen minutes? I don't think so."

"You never know." Tim started back toward the dealership doors. "So, what are you looking for now?"

"I was actually wondering if you had another 2007 Honda Pilot, just like this one, in black." Robert followed him.

"I'll have to look, but it's unlikely. We don't normally have the same car unless it's a Hummer. People have been trading those things in since the economy went down and gas prices went up. You won't believe how many of those suckers we have in stock."

"I bet," Robert answered without listening. He just wanted to get the right car and get out of here.

Tim went behind the counter and started tapping away at the computer, searching for a much-needed item in the system's database.

After a minute, he spoke. "I do have a 2007 Honda Pilot in stock." Tim looked at Robert from behind the counter with questionable eyes as to whether he should continue or not.

"I'll take it," Robert said without question.

"Well, there's a small problem."

"What problem?" Robert said, his stomach churning in anxiety.

"It's not the same color."

"What color is it?"

"It's dark red." The salesman glanced at the computer then back at Robert.

Robert's hope began to fade. "And that's the only one you have?" he asked, more desperately then intended.

Tim started pecking away at the computer again as if something would have changed in the last two seconds. "Yep."

"Dang it." Robert pounded the counter.

"Hey bud, there's no need to get mad."

"Do you have anything else remotely similar to a 2007 Honda Pilot?" he pleaded in desperation.

"It has to be black?"

"Yes, yes, it has to be black."

Tim went away at the computer again, more slowly.

Come on, Robert thought, *give me a break.*

"Well I have a black Envoy, that's the closest we have here in black. It's a very popular color, very corporate I guess."

"I'll take it," Robert said with little hope, as he pulled out his license and proof of insurance. He knew the routine after yesterday's visit.

"Now, I'll need you to look right here so I can take your picture." The man pointed to the computer camera on the top of his monitor.

"What? Why?" Robert asked surprised. "You have my ID."

"It's something Larry has been setting up, making sure you're the same person on your license."

"Can't you just look at me and then the ID?" Robert asked, agitated.

"Look, I just do what I'm told. Now if you want the car, look at this camera and say cheese."

Robert glared into the camera as the salesman clicked the mouse to take the picture. "I'll be right back." He snatched up the contents on the counter. "I have to make copies of these and get your keys and car. If you want, you can sit over there until I bring the Envoy around." He pointed to a bench at the far end of the showroom against a wall where the new Mustang picture was hanging proudly. "It should only take about five minutes."

"Yeah, OK," Robert mumbled, "please hurry though. I don't want to be late for work," he lied.

"I'll be back as soon as I can." Tim disappeared behind a door.

Robert made his way over to the bench, not even glancing at the newest models of cars parked in the showroom.

He loved cars, had since he was a boy. His father used to take him to the race track every year for his birthday. They would go to Toys 'R Us the next day and he'd pick any item he wanted. It was usually a toy car or model he and his father could put together after supper. They would lie out on the rug while his mom cleaned the kitchen, pasting plastic parts together in the living room until a car formed from the pieces.

Robert sat on the bench staring out of the window, waiting for the Envoy to pull around. He had no idea how he was going to explain this to Lindsey. Maybe he could tell her there was an electrical problem with the car and he had to take it back, or the breaks didn't work properly, or the gas pedal stuck. He had gotten used to lying to her, something he wasn't too proud of, but there were a lot of things he wasn't proud of. Two of them happened last night.

A horn honked from outside the window opposite him and the salesman rode up in the black Envoy.

"Finally," Robert said as he made his way out the door.

"Here are the keys." Tim held them out with one hand, "and your ID and insurance." He held these in the other hand. "Do you have anything you need to get out the Honda?"

"Nope," Robert answered as he took his things back.

"Where is the key to the one you're returning?"

"In the car."

"Why did you do that?"

"Look, you got everything you need, right? Can I go?" Robert moved past the man and opened the door.

"You sure can." Tim jumped out the way. "And as always, thank you for choosing Larry's, where finding you the right automotive is our motive," he finished up with his farewell sales routine.

Robert slammed the door, adjusted the seat, and turned the key. He slowly pulled out of the parking lot and made his way back onto the road. He didn't know what he was going to do. He had told Lindsey he might be able to find some work, something that wasn't going to happen.

Robert drove around town careful to avoid the corner of 12th and 5th streets, recollecting his thoughts as he went. A night had gone by since the accident and nothing had happened.

How long should it take for the police to give up if they didn't find evidence proving him guilty? Would he ever feel safe again, or would this ever-pressing constant fear of being found stay with him forever? "What am I going to do? How do I fix this?" he yelled into the steering wheel. *Maybe I should just run away. Then everybody would know something is wrong. They would realize it was me and track me down. I have to go on with my daily life as if nothing happened.* He tried to calm down. "Everything will work out," he reassured himself. "I didn't aim to hit somebody. I should have told the police." He started second guessing his decision. That was the right thing to do. "Ugh!" he screamed out, releasing built up anger and hostility as he beat the dashboard. "Why is this happening to me?"

He pulled off the road into a gas station and parked at the end of the row. He began to cry.

Robert didn't cry often—the last time was at his father's funeral almost five years ago. He sat there at the gas station for an hour, crying, praying, and watching the cars go by.

He started up the Envoy again, pulled out of the station, and headed nowhere in particular until he saw the steeple rising into the sky.

Collins and Jones pulled into the visitor parking lot at Lakeside Memorial Hospital.

"What room is our victim in?" Collins asked as he put the car in park and moved to get out.

"Room 232, Intensive Care Unit," Jones said proudly, finally knowing something Collins asked without second guessing himself.

"All right, let's go." Collins strutted toward the entrance of the hospital. Jones followed in his steps.

They passed through the front door where the smell of the hospital hit them—the lingering odor of sheets and sanitizer.

In the main lobby stood a ten-foot fountain, water constantly trickling down the side. Off to the right sat the receptionist.

"Can I help you?" she asked as Collins made his way toward her.

"I'm Detective Collins, this is my partner Detective Jones, and we're looking for the ICU ward." He flashed his badge, revealing his gun.

She eyed it carefully, a little intimidated, then she said, "Down the hall, take the elevator up to the second floor. Take a left and you should see a sign and arrow pointing you in the right direction," she finished up like she'd been rehearsing all day for that one line.

Collins didn't say anything but turned toward the elevator at the far end of the hall.

"When we get up there," he started as soon as the doors closed, "don't say a word, I'll do all the talking."

Jones stood in silence, nodding in agreement.

The elevator doors opened and Collins took off to the left with big strides. He followed the arrows pointing to the ICU until he found the nurses' station positioned in the middle of the room, facing the patients lying behind glass windows.

"I'm Detective Collins and this is Detective Jones." He flashed his badge again. "We are looking for a…" he looked over at Jones.

"Jaime Mason," Jones answered on cue.

The nurse reached for a clipboard and fumbled through, searching for the name.

"Apparently," she started, "the person of interest is still in surgery and won't be out for a couple of hours. Even then, the doctor wouldn't allow for you to question his patient until tomorrow. I'm sorry gentlemen." She turned to look at the monitor beeping on the left and then walked off toward one of the rooms.

Collins stood there for a second and then whipped around, leading back where he came. He hated wasting time more than anything in the world.

Collins hit the elevator button harder than needed and waited impatiently for the doors to open. Jones was behind him, quiet as a mouse.

The doors sprung open and he walked in, pushing the ground floor button until the elevator closed. When the lift came to a stop, Collins walked out before the doors fully opened. He continued down the hall, past the receptionist desk and the water fountain, taking bigger strides with each step.

Jones hurried after him as he walked toward the car, jumped in, and sped off back to the station.

Robert pulled into a local church parking lot. One he had passed many times but never ventured in. He wasn't really religious, except for Christian holidays and the annual Christmas Day visit. He parked, got out the car, and made his way up the front steps and into the place of worship.

Inside was a small foyer with stairs branching off to the side, leading to an upper deck to view Sunday morning service. Straight ahead was the entrance, which gave way to rows of benches facing the pulpit and choir section at the front of the room. Stained glass windows of saints circled the walls, allowing light to come in, creating a comforting feeling of warmth as Robert walked down the empty aisle. Soft piano music could be heard throughout the room.

Robert sat four rows from the pulpit, not sure what he was doing here. He stared straight ahead, wondering what to say.

"Lord," he began to the empty room. "I'm so sorry. I don't know what to do. I don't know what to say, to make everything OK. It was an accident. It was all my fault. I don't deserve forgiveness but I beg for mercy. Please let everything go away. Take back time. Let me start over. I'll do the right thing this time. I'm so sorry," Robert ended, but didn't move. He kept staring straight ahead while the music played lightly and reassured his decision to come here. He felt better but not quite at ease.

Robert rose and walked up the rows and back into the foyer and out the grand doors. He crossed the parking lot and got into his car and got on the main road. He would have gone by the office if there was something to work on, but business was slow and he didn't feel like it today. His boss encouraged less time in the building—it implied his employees were out earning money. He stopped by a fast food place to pick up some lunch before heading back to the apartment.

Back in the church, the last note played on the CD, which played for several hours during the afternoon. A soft voice came over the intercom. "Thank you for visiting our church. I hope whatever reason brought you here, you find peace when you leave. If you like the soft sounds of the piano music, please pick up a free copy in the choir room. Donations are accepted and all money given will be put back into the church. This is Jaime Mason, the pianist and a devoted member of Sacred Baptist Church, wishing you a blessed day." The CD started back at the beginning as the recorded voice disappeared.

Chapter 6

"What happened to the Honda?" Lindsey asked, trying not to raise her voice as she carried in groceries.

"There was an electrical problem," Robert replied as he moved to help her with the bags.

"What kind of electrical problem?" She gently placed the bags on the counter as she waited for an answer.

"The radio was messing up, the gages on the dashboard weren't working, and the windows wouldn't roll up or down."

"I hope they gave you a discount on the new one—what is it?"

"A 2008 Envoy, and yes they did give me a discount," he added more lies on top of old ones.

He helped her put the can of green beans on the top shelf of the pantry.

"Well good." She smiled as she took out the bread. "Oh great" she moaned.

"What's wrong?"

"The guy at the grocery store put the bread on the bottom. I mean how hard is it to put something light and crushable on top? I know you need a PhD in bagging and it takes years of training to master the art, but really." She held up the smashed loaf for Robert.

"We can fix it." He tried to puff it back up.

"Yeah, right," Lindsey frowned, moving on to the rest of the bags.

"Well maybe we can't, but that doesn't mean we shouldn't try. He was still attempting to reconstruct the whole wheat catastrophe.

"Where did this burst of optimism come from?" she asked as she finished unloading the contents from the plastic bag.

"Just shouldn't give up hope," he tossed the crushed item in the pantry, "on anything."

"Well, I'm glad one of us is hopeful for the future."

Lindsey grabbed the plastic bags and placed them under the sink to use later.

"So what do you think? Macaroni and cheese for dinner tonight? I can even put the apple cinnamon candle on the table and we can pretend we're at that five-star restaurant in the city—what's that place called? Right on 12th street, down a good ways from the school."

"What?" Robert sounded alarmed. "What did you say?"

"I said that restaurant, the five-star one down the street from the school on 12th," she reiterated. "The one we could never afford, with the twenty dollar salads."

"Oh, the umm…oh what is it? I know what you're talking about." His heartbeat slowed. "Diner's Garden."

"That's it. I knew it was something with diner in it. Anyways, so how 'bout it?"

"How 'bout what?"

"Mac and cheese for dinner," she repeated. "I swear you don't listen to anything I say, ever."

"I just didn't hear you," his tone matched hers.

66

"Let's not do this again." She already sounded defeated.

"Sorry, mac and cheese sounds great."

"Good." She did a half smile. "So, any luck with finding some work today?"

"No, it was a false alarm. Jimmy said the deal didn't come through."

Robert turned on the television and went to sit on the couch.

"Well, that's a bummer." She pulled out a pan for the macaroni. "I was hoping to have some extra money. I always feel bad when Krystle gives me a ride to the store. I never have enough gas money to give her for those trips."

"I was hoping to have some extra money for food and clothes," Robert said over the sound of the television.

"Well, yeah, that too." She started pulling out two plates and some silverware. "What are you watching?"

"I was going to see the six o'clock news, but the antenna is messing up again, it's too windy outside." He fingered around with the metal ears, trying to get a better picture and sound.

"Well, dinner will be ready in about ten minutes. What do you want to drink? Water or some generic brand of Pepsi?"

"Water's fine," he called out from behind the TV. "I can't get this stupid thing to work."

Robert fiddled with the television, hoping to find out if something had been reported about last night's hit and run.

"You want to come and put this on the table? It's almost done," Lindsey asked leaning over a boiling pot.

"Yeah, sure."

He gave up on the TV.

"All right, here we go." She turned off the stove with the one working burner, "Dinner is served."

"Smells good."

She grabbed the plates, filling them with noodles and store brand cheese, before sitting with her husband.

"You know, I heard the weirdest thing today. Krystle told me while we were shopping."

"What'd you hear?" Robert asked, not listening, his mind on other things.

"She said there was an accident in front of Jefferson Elementary School last night and the police were all over that place, like a scene from one of those CSI shows."

Lindsey shoved a forkful of macaroni in her mouth.

Robert's attention came full-focus but he kept his voice calm while his heartbeat quickened.

"I know, isn't it weird?" she said between bites. "Why aren't you eating?"

Robert had stopped moving all together.

"What? Oh." He picked up some macaroni and took a bite, not really tasting the food. "Do you know anything else? Was anybody hurt?" he tried sounding nonchalant.

"I don't know, but Krystle told me they ended up taking somebody to the hospital. I don't know their condition. Isn't that awful?" She lifted her water to her mouth. "I mean, can you believe it? Right in front of the school. I hope it wasn't any of the children."

Robert's head was spinning. He was having a hard time keeping his hands and knees steady. He knew this was coming. He had just hoped it was all a terrible dream. Hearing it from Lindsey's voice made it more real than ever.

"Are you all right?" Lindsey looked alarmed.

"Yeah, what? No, I'm fine."

"You're as white as a ghost." Lindsey got up. "Was it the food? It tasted all right to me."

"No, no, it's not the food."

"Then why are you so pale? Do I need to call an ambulance? Are you having a stroke?" She reached out to feel his forehead. "You don't feel warm."

"I think I just need some air. It must have been something I ate for lunch. I tried that Mexican restaurant. They were having a special on churros, so I ate a couple." He got up from the table. "Honestly, I'm fine."

More lies.

He opened the door to the apartment and let the late afternoon air hit his face. He walked down the steps and threw up in the bushes. This moment felt more real to him than the night everything happened. It was all such a blur then—a dream, a nightmare.

He wiped his mouth on the end of his sleeve and staggered back up the stairs, hoping that some color had come back to his face.

He closed the apartment door behind him and went back to the kitchen table where Lindsey sat nervously.

"Are you sure you're all right?"

"I'm fine." He plopped down on the chair.

"I can put that in the fridge and you can eat it later, if you want." She pointed at the mac and cheese.

Robert paused for a moment, wondering if his stomach would handle the food. After a second he gave up on the thought. "Yeah, that would be great."

"All right." She took the plate from the table. She kept a worried eye on him the whole time. "Why don't you lay on the sofa for a little bit, see if that'll help?"

Robert got up from the table and made his way to the couch. He put his feet up and rested his head on a worn pillow. Before he knew it, he was falling asleep. The worries just a few minutes ago had left him for a little while.

"I'm so excited!" Lindsey squealed as she hung up the phone. "That was my mom. She's going to give us her old sofa and dining room table, says she wants to get a new one."

"That's great," Robert agreed from the living room recliner, the Braves playing on the fuzzy screen. "Hey maybe you can get her to throw in a new television set," he added as he went to adjust the antennas, yet again.

"We should spring for cable when we move." Lindsey grabbed an empty box from the kitchen table that Robert had brought back

from the grocery store. *"I know it's a big step, but maybe we could afford the basic channels."*

"Why don't we move in first? Then see about the cable?"

Robert plopped back in his chair.

"I'm just saying, it would be nice." She unloaded the tattered cookbooks from the kitchen shelf that had been given to her by her grandmother, placing them gently in the box.

"I know," Robert said, getting up. *"Here, let me help you with that."* He reached for the pan on the top shelf that was rarely used.

"What about the game?" she asked

"It's almost over. Besides the Braves are up by five. I think it's safe to say they won." He reached for the rest of the antique dishes that were out of Lindsey's arm length.

"Thanks honey." She kissed him on the cheek. *"Did you already call the water guy about the house? Remember, we're moving in on Saturday. I would like to take a hot shower, hopefully with good water pressure,"* she added as she closed the filled box and reached for the tape.

"It's all been taken care of," he reassured her. *"Everything is going to be up and running as far as electricity and water, except for the upstairs bathroom. There is still a broken pipe that needs fixing. Jimmy said he would come by Sunday evening and help with it, so it should be ready Monday."* He placed another empty box that read BOUNTY *on top the counter.*

"Isn't Jimmy helping us move in on Saturday?" she asked, moving to the opposite side of the kitchen, ready to empty the rest of the cabinets of the few dishes they had.

"He can't Saturday. I told you his son has that big game at school."

"He's only in elementary school, how big could it be?" she asked while carefully taking the plates and wrapping them in paper towels and placing them neatly at the bottom.

"It's his son," Robert defended Jimmy as he too took some glasses down and began wrapping them in tissue paper.

"I know, I know," Lindsey said, taking the wrapped glasses Robert had finished and placing them on top the fragile plates. "We could really use his truck though."

"I already talked to him about it and he said we could use it."

"That's great," she beamed, "fewer trips we'll have to make. I do wish we could hire movers or rent a U-Haul." She closed the box and taped it like the first one. "Where's that marker at?"

"Right here." Robert handed her the Sharpie. "And you know we can't afford movers or rent a U-Haul, not if you want to have cable. Besides, we have plenty of cars. Your mom and dad are coming down separately, that's two extra cars, and Charles from work said he'd come down for a couple of hours to help unload the heavy furniture."

"OK," Lindsey gave in as she wrote FRAGILE on the side. She then began another box that read DUNCAN HINES CAKE MIXES. "You told the landlord we were moving, right?"

"Yeah, he's coming by tomorrow to inspect the place, check for any more holes in the wall, and any damages that might have been caused by us. He doesn't want to return our deposit."

Robert helped Lindsey as she moved to the bedroom.

"We can use that money for the cable." Lindsey knelt on the floor to pull the stuff out from under the bed.

"Or food."

"Or food," Lindsey repeated as she pulled out old books that wouldn't fit on her crowded shelf, which was full of cheap makeup. She reached further to find a broken scale, a small heating pad, and a few Christmas decorations.

"So what hotel are your parents staying in?" Robert asked innocently.

"Well, mom's staying at the Holiday Inn, and dad, the Comfort Inn, they're right beside each other," she added, pulling her head from under the mattress.

"Are they going to behave when we move in?"

"We've been living together for a year, oh, and we're married." She mustered a weak laugh.

"That's not what I meant." Robert put the broken scale in the bottom of the box.

"Yeah, they'll be fine. I talked to them about it. I told them if they couldn't get along, I didn't want them here. So they agreed to behave. They both want me out of this crappy apartment as fast as possible."

"Well, I'm glad something good came out of renting this place." Robert moved on to the tangled Christmas lights, tossing them into the box on top the heating pad.

"I know, right." Lindsey was on the other side of the bed taking the drawer out of the bedside table. *"In a way, I'm going to be sad to be leaving this place."*

"You have to be kidding." Robert glanced up at her. *"It brought us nothing but misery."*

"We brought that on each other," Lindsey argued back. *"This was our first home together as husband and wife."*

"Not much of a home," Robert mumbled under his breath, but Lindsey heard him.

"Home is where we are, Robert. It's what we make of it."

"You sound like a Hallmark card. I guess I'm just happy to be leaving this place and the bad times we had in here."

"They weren't all bad." Lindsey strutted over to him with a smirk on her face.

"Well, maybe they weren't all bad." He matched her devious grin.

She leaned into his arms and kissed him as he lifted her up and placed her on the bed, knocking the drawer onto the floor.

"Rise and shine," Lindsey's voice echoed like a distant dream as Robert was slowly waking up, sunlight was coming through the window and beaming into his eyes.

"What?" Robert stretched, groggy.

"Wake up." Lindsey smiled with a small burst of enthusiasm. "Isn't today the big day?" she asked, pulling out cinnamon buns from the fridge.

"Was I here all night?" Robert asked as he rubbed his head. He didn't sleep well.

"You sure were. I tried to get you to come to bed but you wouldn't budge." She reached for a small pan under the stove.

"Sorry about that."

"Don't be. I slept good last night without your constant stirring and snoring or coming in during the middle of the night." She unraveled the cinnamon buns from the container.

"You said something about the big day?" Robert rubbed his eyes again.

"Aren't you showing that house on Fourth Avenue?" She placed the cooking wrack in the oven.

"What? Oh yeah." He'd forgotten about the showing today. A guy named Andrew was thinking about buying a house with his wife, and today they were supposed to be closing the deal. It had completely left his mind.

"Go take a shower and breakfast should be done when you get back."

Lindsey was trying to sound like an eighties sitcom television wife, encouraging her husband as he got ready and went off to work.

He knew she hadn't forgiven him for wrecking the car, but she didn't want to upset him before potentially closing a deal. His salary was small and commission was the meat of his income. If he was in a bad mood, he could lose the deal.

"I laid out your nice suit with the blue tie," she called after him as he made his way toward the bathroom. "Your towel is hanging on the shower."

"Thanks," he hollered as he waited for the water to heat up. He looked in the mirror. He wasn't as pale as last night but he still felt sick to his stomach. His brown hair was a mess and his eyes were weak. His nose was crooked after being broken in a car accident not too many years ago. He stripped down and jumped in the shower, hoping that would wake him as well as wash some of his guilt away.

"Breakfast is ready," he heard Lindsey yell through the door, "it's on the table when you get out."

He didn't answer.

"Can you hear me?" She tried yelling louder as she cracked open the door.

""Yeah, I heard," Robert called back.

"OK."

She shut the door.

He turned the water off, wrapped a towel around him, and stepped out the shower. He dried off and dressed quickly, then walked into the kitchen where Lindsey sat waiting for him.

"You ready?"

"As ready as I'm going to be." He took the cinnamon bun from her hand and took a bite.

"Well, I'm sure you'll do fine," she finished up the conversation.

They sat there silently as he polished off the one cinnamon bun before going back into the bedroom. He draped a tie around his neck, tying it hastily.

"Here let me fix that." Lindsey walked in behind him. "There you go." She stood in front of him, adjusting his tie.

"Thanks," he whispered lowly. He wasn't sure if she heard him. "I'll be back."

He gave her a quick peck on the cheek.

"Well good luck," she murmured.

He could feel her watch him walk from the room.

He grabbed his coat and walked out into the morning air. The showing wasn't for a few hours and he needed space.

He climbed into the Envoy and pulled out of the driveway, coasting toward his office for a few things. The sale was the furthest thing from his mind.

Chapter 7

"Can we talk to the patient today?" Collins asked with half a cup of coffee he bought downstairs.

"What patient would that be?" the nurse asked. She was a different lady then the one he had talked too yesterday. She had a chipper smile on her face.

"Jaime Mason."

Collins glanced around the ICU. He hated hospitals, especially the intensive care unit. He himself had never stayed overnight in one, even after getting shot twenty years ago on the force. After the medic attended him on sight and he was forced to go to the hospital for procedural reasons. He'd gotten up and left after routine tests were done, against doctor recommendations. The bullet went through the top of his right shoulder blade and out the other end, missing any major artery. He still had a nasty scar to prove his war wound—one he wore with pride.

"In that room over there." The nurse pointed across the counter. "The next to last room against the far wall."

Collins heard Jones whisper a "thank you" on his behalf as he scurried behind him.

Collins slid open the door and walked in.

"Sorry to hear about your accident." Collins came around to face the victim. Jaime Mason was lying on the bed, back pressed against the uncomfortable mattress, face turned to the left with a neck brace to keep movement to a minimum. Leg raised in the air, supported by a metal pole.

"If it's all right with you, I'd like to ask you a few questions. I'm Detective Collins and this is Detective Jones."

Jaime nodded in agreement.

"Do you know where you are?" Collins started with the basics.

"Yes."

"Do you know what happened to you?"

"Yes."

"What happened to you?" Collins leaned close to hear.

"I was hit by a car," Jaime struggled to speak.

"Does it hurt to talk?" Collins noticed Jones' look of discomfort in the corner.

A nod.

"I'll try and keep this to a yes and no question then." Collins looked right in the painful eyes of the hospital's newest guest.

"Do you know where you were when this happened?"

"Yes, outside Jefferson Elementary School."

"Do you know who did this to you?"

"No."

"Do you know what time it was?"

Jaime paused and then shook again. Tears were starting to form.

"That's OK," Collins tried to sound sympathetic, but that wasn't him, "I'm almost done."

"Do you know the description of the car?"

"I think an SUV."

"All right, good, good." Collins thought he was getting somewhere.

"Would you be able to recognize it?"

"No."

"OK, thanks." Collins turned to walk away.

"Wait," he heard from the bed.

"Yes?" Collins spun around quickly.

"Do you know if they contacted my daughter?" A wince of pain.

"I don't know, but I'll tell them at the desk." Collins leaned over the bed again, "don't worry, we are going to find the person responsible for doing this to you."

Jaime's expression went blank, as if remembering a distant memory. The panel on the side started beeping and lighting up. The nurse and doctor came swooshing in.

"What are you doing here? Who are you?" the doctor asked Jones who was closest to the door and then he turned on Collins. "What did you do to my patient?"

"We're detectives," Collins said, flashing the badge. "This patient," he spoke with emphasis, "was involved in a hit and run Wednesday night, and we are trying to get to the bottom of it."

"I'm sorry, but I'm going to have to ask you to leave," the doctor said sternly as he began to check the vitals on the patient.

"I was getting ready to. Come on, Jones." He beckoned his finger for him to follow. "We'll be back soon."

81

"We need you to breath slowly and bring your heart-rate down," Collins heard the doctor say as he was leaving the room, "we can't have the bleeding on the brain start up again, not with the other condition." That was the last thing he heard as he walked from the ICU, down the hall toward the elevator.

"Come on." Collins pushed the elevator door as he turned to Jones, "we're going to the crime scene."

Jones didn't say a word but followed reluctantly into the elevator, afraid to mention anything about what just happened in the other room.

Robert took the long way to his office. He gathered enough courage to drive by the school where the accident took place. His heart pounded harder, causing him trouble catching his breath.

Only three blocks away.

"This is it."

There it was, no yellow tape like he'd imagine. From a distance, there was nothing to suggest anything had happened here. He drove slower. There were a few skid marks from when he slammed on the brakes and a couple of dark spots on the edges of the curb, where the victim bled out on the sidewalk. That, along with the tire marks, would disappear soon enough.

This will all vanish in time, Robert thought, his heart pounding less, his breathing becoming normal. He sped off in the direction of his office, feeling slightly better.

There weren't any cars on either side of the road, just one coming down opposite him on the intersection, which stopped at a red light. Robert put the pedal down when the light changed and drove off toward his destination ten miles away. He tried to push everything from his mind and focus on the task in front of him.

Jones sat quietly in the passenger seat as Collins flew toward the crime scene. There wasn't any music playing. The wind attacked the car as it swerved in and out busy lanes. Jones' uneasy breathing emitted from the passenger seat.

"I hate traffic," Collins muttered under his breath.

Jones sat quietly.

Collins wondered why this kid didn't speak. He knew he was intimidating. He didn't make nice with people and he enjoyed the silence.

They sat in awkward peace most of the trip.

Collins slowed to a halt at a stoplight.

"Why aren't these things on motion sensors?"

He looked around, waiting for green freedom. The only other car was opposite him on the other side of the intersection—a black Envoy.

The light turned green and the SUV took off in a hurry.

Collins didn't pay any mind to the driver as he sped up and stopped once again, this time at a stop sign, then once more in front of the school.

****

Robert walked through the doors of his office. The two-story building resided in the only part of the town still flourishing under the economic struggle, especially for Happy Homes Realtor. He passed by the receptionist, who was playing solitaire on the computer while popping on some gum.

"Hello, Mr. Armes" she said out of courtesy.

"Wyndi," he replied. Their normal routine.

Robert walked up the steps and passed by a few doors of his co-workers and competition, onto the open floor with cubicles. Robert strolled down the rows into his familiar squared depression of employment.

"Are you ready for the sale?" Charles asked over the cubicle wall.

"Yeah, I hope so," Robert replied as he put his briefcase on the table and woke his computer up.

"What time's the showing?"

"One thirty."

"Do you think you'll get this one?"

"I hope so," Robert said, annoyed. He hadn't been able to close a sale for a while now, and everything was riding on this deal.

"Are we on for next week?"

"What?" Robert asked confused.

"You and Lindsey, Suzanne and me, bowling. Remember? It's half-off Wednesday Bowl-O-Rama for two hours at the alley."

"Oh, yeah. How is Suzanne—still pregnant?"

"Yep," Charles said enthusiastically, "can't believe it's been two months already. Seven more and I'm going to be a father."

"I'm happy for you," Robert said as he browsed through the documents on the screen.

"Don't tell Lindsey, we were going to tell you and her Wednesday, but I can't wait."

"What is it?" Robert turned to face his oldest friend. They had gone to school together and joined the company one year apart from each other.

"We would be honored if you and Lindsey would be the godparents to our child."

"What?" Robert's jaw dropped and then a small smile appeared. "I don't know what to say. Are you sure?"

"Yeah, we're sure. You and Lindsey are always so happy together. Our potential son or daughter would be lucky to grow up in such a loving environment."

If only he knew what was happening behind closed doors, Robert thought. "We would be honored."

"Now you have to act surprised when Suzanne brings it up on Wednesday. She would be mad at me if she knew I ruined the surprise for her."

Robert's jaw dropped in reenactment. "Is this good?"

"Perfect." Charles laughed. "Put you in front of a judge and you could lie about murder with that look. 'I swear I don't know what you are talking about, you've got the wrong guy.'" Charles mimicked what he figured an authoritative person would sound like.

Robert's jaw dropped even further. His stomach churned and the room started to spin.

"Now you're taking it too far." He laughed even harder.

"I'll do better when it counts," Robert mustered a weak laugh.

"Listen up everybody." Austin, Robert's boss, walked through the door into view of the semi-busy room.

"What now?" Charles whispered to Robert as he turned to rush off to his cubicle to pretend to work hard on something important for the organization.

"As most of you know, or for those who attended the Woman's Health fundraiser this past Wednesday through Thursday, it was a big success. Now I can't say for certain how much the fundraiser brought in, but I think it's safe to say at least five thousand dollars was raised."

A small, unenthusiastic clap met the brief silence Austin had paused for.

"I am proud to say our company donated fifty dollars during the walk-a-thon when we sponsored Jaime Mason, who walked a little over five miles."

Robert was paying little attention. He hit the print button for the document he would need during his sale.

"Congratulations to all who participated," Austin said before leaving for his office.

"You want to grab an early lunch before you have to leave for your presentation?" Charles appeared again as soon as his boss left.

"Yeah, sure," Robert replied. "McDonald's OK with you?"

"I'm loving it," Charles replied.

****

"What are we doing here?" Jones asked.

"We are here to solve a crime."

Collins was a little surprised he spoke first.

"All the evidence and preliminary findings and bulk of information are at the station. What are we going to find here that the crime scene investigators missed?" Jones glanced at his watch.

"The truth about what happened here the other night. You got somewhere to be?"

"Not for a couple of hours."

"Well, I'm glad you have time to spare, now look around," Collins said tersely.

"What am I looking for?"

Jones fanned the ground.

"Anything," Collins replied vaguely as he canvassed the area then glanced up at the school. "Does that building have cameras on the roof top?"

"I don't know." Jones looked up. "I'll find out."

"Hold on," he said as Jones was starting to take off toward the school. "We need to finish here."

"What are we looking for?" Jones repeated.

"I told you, evidence," Collins' tone had sharpened. "Do you have the case report with you?"

"It's in the car."

Collins eyed every detail of the scene carefully. "What does it say?" he asked as Jones appeared beside him, folder in hand.

He flipped through the crime scene pictures and written descriptions scribbled by someone in a hurry. "Broken glass, lots of blood, not much else. The medics came and found Mason faced down on the pavement next to the curb," he pointed in the direction based on the picture.

"There's nothing else?" Collins looked irritated.

"No, sir." Jones double checked. "Only that the victim was barely conscious and incoherent."

"What about skid marks?" Collins asked as he eyed some tire prints on the road.

"No, sir."

"Go get the camera."

Collins was studying the ground with intensity.

Jones ran back to the car, grabbed the camera, and snapped a few rounds of the marks on the pavement.

"If it's not two inches from the victim," Collins raised his head, "nobody notices."

"How do you know those tire prints belonged to the driver of our hit and run? Isn't it more likely someone slammed on breaks because a kid ran out in the road?"

"So we should just dismiss it? Assume that's what happened. Let me ask you something. What if you're wrong? What if these are the very tire prints of the vehicle that caused someone to end up in a hospital? I guess we should just guess?"

"Sorry sir," Jones hastily stammered. "I didn't mean...I just thought...What are the chances?"

"That's what you are going to find out."

Collins walked toward the car.

"All right, we got half of what we came for."

"Half?"

"Yes, the other is at the school."

"The cameras?" Jones looked skeptical. "Even pointing in the right direction, that far away, and at night, there's no way to get a facial recognition."

"That may be, but the report said the nine-one-one call came from a payphone outside."

"Yeah."

"Come on Jones, use your head."

The car rolled to a stop. They both got out.

"The assailant would have come by the school to make the call."

"You have to use common sense, son." Collins pushed open the doublewide doors of Jefferson Elementary and made his way to the office.

"Excuse me," he tapped on the empty desk, "anyone here?"

"Yes," came a small voice from around the corner, "can I help you?"

An elderly woman in her fifties popped into view. She had small wrinkles around her eyes that were partially covered by small-rimmed glasses. She wore a blue blouse and skirt that followed her legs down to her ankles. She had a bright smile with yellow teeth, evidence she'd smoked a lot in her youth.

"Detective Collins and Jones, we are investigating the hit and run outside on the street."

"Oh my gosh, what happened? It wasn't a child, was it?"

"No, it wasn't. Now we don't have a lot of time."

"Yes, what can I do for you gentlemen," she asked, wide-eyed.

"Do you have cameras on the outside of this building?"

"Unfortunately, no, the school board didn't feel it prudent under the circumstances. Now the high school owns at least twenty of them on each end of the building. That place is more like a delinquent center than an educational institute. I tell you, I don't know what the world is coming to," she sighed softly.

"Well, I bet the school board feels stupid about their decision now."

A brief pause.

"We do however, have cameras in the front hallway coming in, if the person you're looking for was within line of sight of the front door, you may have something," she added hopefully, wanting to help.

"We will take it," he said, unenthused.

"It'll take a few minutes. I have to call the principal and get authorization since you don't have a warrant. You don't have a warrant do you?"

"No."

"Then it'll take about ten minutes, please have a seat." She pointed to a worn red sofa that had been through more than its share of wear and tear over the years. "I'll be right back."

She disappeared back the way she came.

Collins wandered to the couch but didn't sit. He gazed in the mirror, looking at his reflection. He was tall, about six foot, brown hair with more gray than brown. His hazel eyes held many stories of someone who had lived an adventurous—but lonely and troublesome—life.

He inhaled and exhaled slowly then walked out the office. Jones followed out of habit.

"What are we doing?" he asked as Collins walked the hallway opposite the entrance to the building.

"I'm looking for the camera." He searched the ceiling. It hung halfway down the hall. *What kind of elementary school needed cameras?* he wondered. He knew they were standard for every school within the district, put in motion by the new mayor in order to make parents, faculty, and kids feel safe. But an elementary school? Was that really necessary?

Collins stood behind the camera facing the direction the lenses pointed. It was a straight line toward the door.

Jones stood against the wall trying to stay out the way.

The elderly woman from the office poked her head out the door into the hallway looking for her visitors.

"Detectives." She waved her arms as if they couldn't see her. "I've been given permission. Here is the tape." She threw up her left arm. "It didn't take as long as I thought it would."

Collins and Jones walked toward her, "Thank you." Collins acquired the tape. "We will get this back as soon as possible."

"Don't worry about it." She waved her arms as if refusing the words. "All the cameras are hooked up to a computer mainframe and DVD/VCR. This enables us to retrieve a hard copy on demand as well as store an extra copy on the computer. Now I don't know how it works or even what that means, but the man who set it up could go on for hours if you asked him." She flashed her yellow teeth in a smile that had taken place out of habit.

"OK, well thanks again." He held out his hands to shake hers.

"Judy," she said, clutching her hand over his.

"Judy." He released her grip and made his way toward the exit.

"I hope you find the man responsible for this. That's just awful, hitting someone alone with a car is bad enough. Then not even having the courtesy to turn yourself in," she yelled after the detectives as Collins and Jones walked through the main doors.

"Don't you have a thing to do?" Collins asked Jones as they got in the car.

"Yes sir, I'm supposed to be meeting my wife in an hour for some—" but he got cut off again.

"I didn't ask what you were going to do. I asked if you had something you needed to do."

He started the engine.

"Yes, sir." Jones buckled his seatbelt.

"When we get back to the station, go ahead and do whatever it is you need to do, but I expect you back as soon as it's over. I don't care if it's ten o'clock at night."

"Yes, sir" Jones reiterated. "What about the tape?"

"Like I said." Collins pulled out onto the road. "I don't care if it's ten o'clock at night."

Chapter 8

"Welcome." Robert held out his hands to greet the couple coming up the walkway. "It's nice to see you again, Geraldine, Andrew." He shook their hands. "Now, we all know today is a big day," Robert put on his best sales face, "but I want you to be sure this is what you want, so take all the time you need—walk through the house, look it over, ask any questions you may have. I'll be in the kitchen when you're done."

Geraldine and Andrew thanked Robert as they walked into the living room and up the stairs.

Robert always hated the part before the signing. Even after weeks of showing the same house over and over to the same people, and after the work was done and papers were drawn up, the buyers always felt the need to walk through the house again before they signed their names on the dotted line. As if something might have drastically changed the few days they weren't there.

Robert went over to the kitchen's counter top and rested against the marble finish. He laid out the papers and pens, ready for a signature as soon as the couple was done.

He started to sweat a little. He never sweated during the closing end of a sale, but the thought of the accident kept flashing through his mind, over and over. Robert reached up to turn on the fan, hoping the gentle breeze would cool him down.

"Everything all right?" he asked as Geraldine and Andrew came down the steps.

"So far so good." Andrew smiled at his wife as they moved toward the back portion of the downstairs.

"Well, I'm here when you're done," Robert called after them as they disappeared behind a door. *Come on*, he thought, tapping the pen against the table.

They appeared out of the dining room, grins on their faces.

"Are you ready, honey?" Andrew asked as they held hands walking across the room toward the kitchen.

"I think so," she said with a grin from ear to ear.

"This really is a beautiful place," Robert started his closing lecture. "Not only is there a new stove, hardwood floors, and let's not forget that new house smell," he conjured up a smile, but his mind wondered to the house he bought out in the country.

It didn't hold a candle to this place. He could never afford something like this.

He continued on, "the neighborhood is wonderful and this really is the best deal in town. So if you're ready," he held out a pen, "just sign by the X's and we'll get this filed away and you two will become brand new homeowners."

"All right, here we go." Andrew held the pen firmly in his hand. "There's no going back after this." He smiled again at his wife.

They were so young, so in love. Robert couldn't help but think how they were the complete opposite of him and Lindsey.

"Just do it." Geraldine nudged at her husband. "Come on, Detective."

She pushed his arm toward the paper.

"You're a detective?" Robert asked, his heart pounded and his palms began to sweat.

"Sure am." Andrew looked up at Robert. "Just got a job not too long ago, actually."

"Really?" Robert tried to sound more surprised than scared. He could feel the color starting to drain from his face.

"Come on, sign the paper." Geraldine nudged at his arm again.

"Andrew," Andrew read the signing out loud.

"Detective," his wife chimed in with a smile.

"Haha." He grinned at her. "I don't think I can write that."

"I know, I'm just so proud of you." Geraldine kissed his cheek.

Come on, Robert was screaming in his head, *sign the paper so I can get the hell out of here.*

"OK." Andrew started up where his pen left off. "Andrew Taylor Jones" he spoke out loud as he signed with a ballpoint pen. "A proud home owner," he said, handing the pen to his wife.

When they were done, Robert quickly scribbled his name where he needed to seal the deal.

"OK," Robert rushed his words. "Here is your copy, this is mine. I'll file this right away. Here are your keys and thank you for choosing Happy Homes as your realtor contractor," he finished up with the company's motto, his words almost to the point of incomprehension.

Robert grabbed up his things in a hurry, shoved the papers back into his briefcase, and took off out the front door. He had to get away.

****

Collins was sitting behind his desk watching the footage, over and over. There was a lot of activity in the school that night during the time of the accident, blocking the view of the door.

Who has a banquet this late? he wondered, becoming more impatient every time he had to rewind the tape so he didn't miss anything.

"Here, you look through this."

Collins popped out the tape and tossed it to Andrew, who'd just walked in.

"Right away."

He walked toward his desk and slid the movie in the machine.

"What are you smiling at?" Collins inquired. He was taking his frustration out on Jones.

"Sorry, me and the Mrs. just bought a house together." The smile fell a little.

Collins thought back to when he and his wife bought their first home and how happy they were. "You'll be paying for that investment long after your dead."

Jones didn't say anything. He just rewound the tape a few minutes before the 911 call came in. "Sure were a ton of people there that night."

"Now find the right one," Collins grunted as he logged onto his computer.

"Wait a second," Jones said after ten minutes. He sounded excited, like he'd spotted something. "What's that there?" He pointed to the dimly lit screen.

Collins rose from his desk and made his way toward Andrew. "What?"

He rewound the screen. "Right there." Jones pointed as he paused the tape again.

"I don't see nothing," Collins argued. It was getting harder for him to notice smaller details with constant worsening eyesight.

Andrew hit the rewind button for the second time. "Right there." He pointed to the same spot. "That dark image. It's only there for a split second as it crosses the door."

"Can you clean it up, or take the people out of the way, or zoom in or something?"

"It'll take a couple of minutes, I'll have to transfer the video to the computer, then digitize the image and—"

"I don't care how you do it," Collins barked. "Just do it, now." He walked back to his desk to finish what he started on the computer. He pulled up the DMV camera database.

There was something he'd noticed when he went to the crime scene. With any luck, they might have caught a break. He punched in his access code and typed the time he wanted to view.

The victim said there was a car, an SUV that caused the hospital visit. Maybe, if the vehicle came through that stoplight, they could sift through images using the search criteria Jaime provided and find a match.

Collins viewed the intersection. Even as late as it was, there was traffic coming through the junction.

Collins rubbed his brow, thinking. "The way those skid marks were positioned on the road and location the body was found, the suspect would have been traveling west."

Collins closed the cameras pointing in the wrong direction and focused on the ones heading toward the school, eliminating any sports cars or small sedans that past through.

He adjusted the time of the surveillance footage thirty minutes prior to the 911 call and watched as ten vehicles went through the light.

There were four SUVs.

Collins wrote down the license plate numbers of the one closest to the time of the incident, working his way backwards.

"Sir," Jones hesitated at his desk. "I compressed the image best I could with the software on these computers."

"Did you get a face?"

"Not exactly," Andrew answered, afraid to say more.

"Well?" Collins walked to Jones' desk.

"Well," Andrew started, "the person didn't face the camera directly. The only thing I can tell is the suspect's Caucasian. Other than that, it's my best guess."

"That's not good enough," Collins said, hitting the desk with his fist. "Here." He handed Jones the list of license plate numbers. "You can do this faster than I can. I want the names and addresses of all these people here."

"Yes, sir."

Jones took the list from his hand.

"Once you are done, cross reference them with body shops within a fifty-mile radius. Check for frontal damages."

"Yes, sir," Jones repeated as he pecked away ferociously on the keyboard.

Robert drove around town, sweat pouring down his face. "Calm down. The detective didn't know anything. Otherwise, I would be in handcuffs instead of on the highway." He took in a deep breath. "Everything is going to be OK, I'm OK."

Robert continued driving for about an hour until his heartbeat was under control and he'd stopped sweating. He pulled onto the familiar street he reluctantly called home. Lindsey would be waiting inside to hear the good news. He parked the car, slowly got out, and marched to the door.

"How did it go?" Lindsey asked as he walked in.

"I got it." Robert tried to sound more excited than he felt.

"That's wonderful."

Lindsey gave him a kiss.

"Yeah," was all Robert could say.

"How much money are we getting?"

"I don't know. I have to file the paperwork and wait."

Robert fell into the kitchen chair.

"How much do you think you're going to get?" she pestered him.

"I don't know."

"Why aren't you as excited as me?" Lindsey looked a little worried.

"I am excited." Robert tried to beam a smile.

"You didn't make the sale, did you?"

"No, I got it."

"Don't lie to me. If you closed the deal, you would be all smiles, jumping up and down, happy as a clam. Now did you make the sale?"

"Honey, I made the sale. I just don't feel good, that's all." Robert looked at her with weak eyes.

"Are we still going out to celebrate? I was thinking we could go to Onion Rings in town and have a cheap dinner. Continue the celebration. Plus, I could really go for something new with the money you're going to be getting from this sale. You think we could?"

"I don't know," Robert complained.

"Robert, please. We never do anything romantic anymore."

"Lindsey, we don't have the money."

"I babysat the kid down the street today. Their usual nanny canceled on them for some reason or another. Anyways, they called me after you left and I said I would fill in. I made thirty dollars today. We could use that. Come on, if you don't go, I'll go by myself."

"Ugh."

"Robert Armes, you are coming with me tonight."

"Fine."

"Give me ten minutes," Lindsey said as she moved toward the bathroom.

Twenty minutes later, Lindsey was ready. Together they walked out into the brisk nighttime air.

"Nice car," Lindsey said after a few minutes of silent driving toward the restaurant. "What did you say was wrong with the other one?" she asked, desperately trying to start a conversation.

"Electrical," Robert mustered—his thoughts back to Andrew and his sale.

"Sheesh. Your luck with cars."

Another minute of silence.

"Hopefully, if things go well, I can babysit for the neighbors more often. They weren't too happy with the cancellation at the last minute from the girl who normally watches their kid."

"Uh, huh."

"If that's true, we could be making an extra hundred bucks a week."

"Yep." Robert wasn't paying attention. *Does this mean the police have no leads?* he wondered.

"Are you listening to me?"

"What, yeah, a hundred bucks, that's great," Robert said as his mind kept thinking about the possibility of not being found out by the detective.

"Pull in here." Lindsey pointed to an empty parking spot near the front. "They aren't that busy. Maybe we won't have to wait long for a table."

They jumped out the car and walked toward the entrance.

"Table for two," Robert said to the maître d'.

"Right this way," the unenthusiastic man from behind the podium said as he led the couple through a dimly lit dining area. "Your waiter will be with you shortly." He laid the menus on the table and disappeared back to his post, dragging his feet the whole way.

"This is nice." Lindsey tried again to start a conversation.

"Yep," Robert said glancing through the menu without reading the items. *What if the police never find a suspect?* His mind was racing with hopeful possibilities.

"Hi, I'm Katelyn and I'll be your server today." The waitress showed up with an enthusiastic grin. "What would you lovebirds like to drink?"

"Pepsi," Lindsey said

"Same here," Robert replied without looking up from the menu.

"Be back in a second." The waitress left to retrieve the beverages.

"So tell me about your sale," Lindsey said.

"Not much to tell." Robert placed his menu down.

"Oh come on." She leaned closer to the table. "Tell me how you convinced the buyers to purchase the house."

"I showed it to them, they liked it, that's it."

"Come on Robert, I'm trying here."

"I'm sorry. I guess I still don't feel well."

"Do you want to go back home?" Lindsey asked, upset.

"No, we're here now. Let's eat something."

"Here you go." The waitress returned with the drinks. "Have you decided on what you would like to eat?"

"I'll have the daily special," Lindsey answered.

"Me too," Robert replied.

"Wow, I wish all my customers were as easy to please as you two," Katelyn said as she wrote the order down. "Let me take those menus for you." She reached for the menus. "Be back soon with your meal." She turned to leave.

"Excuse me." A busboy bumped into Katelyn one table over from Robert and Lindsey.

"Don't worry about it, Jesse."

"What are you still doing here? I thought your shift ended an hour ago?"

"It did, but my replacement never showed up."

"Who was supposed to relieve you?"

"Jaime."

"That's unusual. Mason is never late."

"I know, I'm starting to worry."

"The only reason Jaime took this job was to pay for medical bills."

"How can one person work a forty-hour work week at another place, plus this job?"

"I know what you mean. I hate doing thirty sometimes."

"I feel ya. Well, I've got to get these orders in before I'm fired," Katelyn said.

The waitress returned with their meal and they both ate in silence. There wasn't much to say, and Robert's mind was on other things. Forty minutes later, Lindsey and Robert were finished with their dinner and on their way home.

"Well that was nice," Lindsey said as she entered the apartment.

"Sure was." Robert tried sounding happy. "I'm going to go lie down and see if I feel better."

"I'll put your leftover food in the fridge and bring you some aspirin."

Robert stumbled to the bedroom. He face-planted into the sheets. Thoughts of the accident were racing through his mind, bouncing around his skull. His head throbbed. He felt too weak to move.

Robert had been fine earlier. He'd made the sale, went by the accident, and felt less pain about what happened there. Why now did he feel different? He was two inches away from a detective and shook hands with the man who had no idea Robert was involved in a crime. That should be a good thing—they weren't on to him. He should feel relieved. Misery was all that filled the empty hole inside him.

Lindsey walked in the room with water and two white pills. She handed them to Robert.

"Feel better honey." She rubbed his head and quietly left.

He swallowed the drugs with no help from the water, and tossed and turned in bed, waiting for the aspirin to work. Hours passed. The same thoughts kept flashing through his mind until he fell into an uneasy sleep.

"Are you ready kiddo?" Greg hugged his little girl as he stepped from his jeep.

"Almost," she answered him, all smiles about the big day. "We've got a few things we have to stick in your car. Mom is driving the Honda, and Jimmy's truck is full. You're the last one to the party."

"Just like always." Irma popped her head around the car to put her two cents in.

"Come on, mom," Lindsey turned around, "you promised you'd be nice."

"Sorry, sweetie," she apologized, glaring at Greg. "It's true though."

"Mom!"

Robert finished strapping the bungee cords on the truck to keep the mattress from falling.

"We may have to make two trips." He spotted his father-in-law. "Greg, glad you could come. Thanks for the help. We sure need it."

"Happy to do it." Greg shook his hand. "What do I need to take?"

"Those boxes." Robert pointed at the edge of the steps. "I'll help you load them."

Robert and Greg quickly packed down the Jeep Cherokee with boxes while Lindsey double-checked the locks on the apartment door.

"Good to go," she called out as she jumped the two steps from the porch to the grass in excitement. "Let's do this."

"Everyone's following me, right?" Robert asked while the group went to their separate cars.

"Yeah," they chimed in chorus. Robert couldn't help but laugh.

"All right, then. I'm going to take it slow."

"Let's go, grandma," Greg shouted out.

"Speaking of…" Irma rolled down her car window, "when are we…"

"Not now." Lindsey rolled her eyes at her mother, who was always bothering her about when she planned on having children.

The caravan loaded up and headed out toward the country home, slow but steady.

Robert was in the lead and in control.

"Hello?" Robert answered his phone in a whisper as he crawled out of bed, Lindsey softly breathing beside him.

Silence

"Hello?" he repeated louder.

Nothing.

"Whoever this is, if you don't—"

"Rebecca," a familiar voice on the other end spoke and he couldn't quite place it.

"Rebecca who?" he asked as he made his way toward the kitchen.

A brief pause came from the other end.

"Hello?"

"Is this Robert?" the woman questioned, "Robert Armes?"

"Who is this?" Robert sounded alarmed. "How did you get my number?"

"You gave it to me."

Robert fell back against the counter. "No, I didn't. I'm hanging up."

"Wait!" The voice rang through his end of the phone. "From Ohio. We met at the bar. We went back to my hotel."

Robert lost his breath and his heart jumped from his chest. The room started to spin. He grabbed the edge of the counter for support, his knuckles turning ghost white along with the color in his face. "What? Why are you calling me?"

"I need..." Rebecca paused. "I need you."

"What?" Robert's alarm went to panic. His wife was in the other room. "Look. That was a one-time thing. I never should have given you my number. Don't call me again!" He moved to hang up but the same pleading word prevented him from doing so.

"Wait, that's not what I meant. I need your help. Please," her voice choked up.

He imagined her holding back tears.

"What? What is it?" Robert heard himself say.

"I need someone to go with me to the hospital."

Oh, God, Robert thought. "The hospital? Did you give me a...a disease?"

"No, no, nothing like that," Rebecca started, but she broke down on the other end.

"Finish what you called me to say."

Robert didn't have time for this.

"I need you to go with me to the hospital—my mother, she's dying."

All Robert could hear were sobs. "I don't know what you want me to do? I don't even know you. Don't you have some friends you can call? Perhaps a brother, father, the guy you get your coffee from in the morning? Anybody else." Robert knew what he said was harsh, but he didn't have a choice, not with everything else.

"I'm an only child," Rebecca managed to spit out through tears. "My father, he's..." she paused, "not around and I don't know anyone here."

"You don't even know me." Robert argued.

"You're the only one I do know."

"But you were here for a month. You didn't make any friends, any colleagues, nothing?"

"I lied to you earlier."

"What?" Robert was upset, even though he lied to her too. He couldn't help it. "You lied to me?" His voice grew louder. "How do I know you're not lying now?"

All he heard were more tears on the other end, which reassured the truth.

"All right, all right," he tried saying with a little compassion. "Where is she?"

"She's in a hospital. I just received the call a few minutes ago," Rebecca whispered into the phone, choking back more tears.

"What hospital?"

"Lakeside Memorial Hospital."

Robert's heart began to pound again. That would be the same hospital the ambulance would have taken his victim.

"I don't know..." Robert tried to back out.

"Please," Rebecca pleaded.

"What happened to her?" he asked.

"I don't know, they wouldn't give me specifics over the phone." Rebecca started talking fast. "Apparently, she's been in and out of the hospital for a few months now, and this time it doesn't look good."

"Oh," was all Robert managed to utter.

"Can I come to your place?"

"Umm..." Robert fumbled for a good excuse. "My place, uh, why don't we just meet at the hospital?"

"How do I know you'll show?"

"I stayed on the phone this long, haven't I?"

Lindsey stirred in the other room. "Look, I've got to go. I'll meet you in the hospital parking lot. Look for my car."

"Honda Pilot, right?"

"What? No. A 2008 Envoy, black."

"What happened to your Honda?"

"I'll meet you at one." And with that, Robert hung up the phone just as Lindsey opened the bedroom door.

"Who was that?" Lindsey asked as she rubbed her eyes.

"Good news, honey," Robert tried sounding excited. "Jimmy thinks he's got some work for me this afternoon."

"Oh, good, at one?" she asked while reaching for a bowl in the cabinet.

"What? Yeah, at one," Robert agreed as he retrieved the milk.

"That's wonderful honey." She grabbed the corn flakes from on top the fridge. "Do you want some?" She reached for another bowl.

"No. I'm going to take a shower and file those papers from yesterday."

"Glad you're feeling better honey. Hold on though." She poured some corn flakes and added milk. "I was thinking, maybe Jimmy could help me find a job too. It's not fair you have to carry the financial burden on your own. Plus, I don't know if that babysitting job is going to come through. I haven't heard back from the neighbors yet. What you said the other night really got to me. I want to help. Maybe I'll call him this afternoon."

"No," Robert said defensively.

"What?" Lindsey looked alarmed, "Why?"

"I just..." Robert searched for the right words. "I don't want you to bother him for a job when he's trying to help me. I'll mention it to him later."

"OK."

Lindsey sat down at the table. "I'll take anything," she added as Robert disappeared into the bedroom.

Great, another problem, he thought as he took a quick shower.

Robert got dressed and walked back into the kitchen where Lindsey was reading a newspaper.

"Did you spend money on that?" he asked, tying his tie.

"No, it's from last week. The neighbors across the street gave it to me. I told them I would recycle it." She took a bite of her corn flakes. "I like reading the comics and looking through the job listings to see if anything's available."

"Oh." Robert wasn't really listening. "I'll be back."

"Why are you all dressed up if Jimmy works in construction?"

"I want to look my best. I have a change of clothes in the car," Robert lied.

"Good luck," she yelled after him as he walked through the door.

He had five hours before meeting with Rebecca at the hospital, and he needed to get to the office and file those papers.

Chapter 9

Robert pulled into his usual parking spot at the office. It was Saturday, and the place was half-empty. He opened the double glass doors and made his way inside and up to his cubicle. The receptionist was gone. Robert sat down at his desk and began the tedious final paperwork when he heard his name bellowed out across the room.

"Robert!" his boss yelled across the floor. "In my office now!"

What did I do? Robert thought as he reluctantly rose from his desk and walked toward the manager's office.

"Robert, ole boy," Austin said as his employee walked through his doors. "How's it going?" He didn't leave time for a response. "Did you get the sale?"

"I sure did," Robert replied, relief swept over him.

"That a boy."

"Thank you, sir."

"How long have you been with the company, son?"

"Ever since college." Robert took a seat opposite Austin.

"Well, I was a little worried about you. You haven't had much revenue coming in for a while now."

"I know, it's tough times out there."

"I hear ya. I hated having to lay off some of your co-workers, but it was a necessity I had to do for our company to survive these economic times."

"No one blames you, sir," Robert lied. Everyone blamed him, even if it wasn't his fault. No one wanted to lose their job.

"Well you're probably wondering why I called you in here."

"A little bit, sir" Robert answered, shifting in his seat.

"I hate to tell you this, but unless I see some significant improvement in your sales and overall performance here, I'm going to have to let you go. Now I don't want to do that because I know you have a wife to take care of, but if you don't succeed, I don't succeed and everyone loses. You understand?"

"Yes, sir."

"I'm giving you a two-month grace period where you will have to double your earnings or else it's the door."

"Yes, sir."

"I like you, Robert, I want you to flourish here, but I need to know you will put forth the effort."

"I will, sir."

"Good man."

"Thank you, sir."

"All right, well that'll be it. Please shut the door on the way out."

"Yes, sir."

Robert left and went back to his cubicle. *Great, another thing to worry about.* He thought about the possibility of losing his job while working on the paperwork, until it was time to meet Rebecca at the hospital.

****

"All right." Jones walked over to Collins. "I've got one suspect."

"What are you waiting for?" Collins asked, looking up at Jones, who stopped talking.

"Oh," Jones said, flustered, as he handed the printout to Collins. "The man you are looking at is a school teacher—a Mr. Dave Robertson. He works at the high school but lives only two blocks away from the elementary school. I called the local body shops and it turns out his car was taken in a day after the accident, with frontal damage. None of the other leads panned out."

"Sounds like our guy." Collins got up from his desk and grabbed his jacket. "Got the address?"

"Yes, sir."

"Let's go." Collins strutted toward the door, Jones right behind him.

Robert pulled into Lakeside Memorial Hospital's visitor parking lot. He wasn't quite sure what he was doing here. He knew he'd promised Rebecca he would be here, but he could still blow her off.

Robert waited like he said he would. *The body I put in the hospital could be here too.* The thought kept bouncing around his brain.

He took off his wedding ring and stuffed it in the middle console, taking a deep breath to relieve some fear and anxiety.

There was a quick tap on the side window. He jumped. It was a familiar face—one that had no doubt been crying ever since he hung up with her hours ago. She looked awful.

"Rebecca." He got out the car and hesitated before putting his arms around her.

"I can't believe you came." She looked at him with red, puffy eyes.

"I told you I would." Robert sounded sympathetic. "You ready to go see her?"

"Yeah," she said, muffled.

Robert led her toward the front entrance, noticing a huge waterfall fountain as he walked in.

"Do you know what room she's in?" he asked, glancing over at the receptionist.

Rebecca nodded.

Robert understood being upset about a parent, but this was a little too much for him. "What floor?" he asked, guiding her into the elevator.

"Second." She tried to gather herself.

Robert pushed the button, and the elevator doors closed. "I'll wait outside the room while you go in."

"No, no, I want you with me, please. I don't think I can handle this by myself." She reached for his hand.

"OK," Robert said, his heart thumping hard. The thought of someone lying somewhere in this very hospital because of him was too much. It took all his strength not to turn around and run out the hospital.

The elevator doors opened onto the second floor. "This way." She led Robert down the hall. She slowed down as they neared her mother's room.

"Are you ready?" Robert asked, squeezing her hand for comfort.

Rebecca didn't look at him or even acknowledge they were holding hands as she pushed open the door and walked in the room. She gasped at the sight of her mom lying in a hospital bed.

"Oh, Mom. I'm so sorry." She let go of Robert as she leaned over her mother's bed. "Mom? She started to cry again. "I'm so sorry. I'm sorry for everything. Everything that happened. Everything that went wrong, it's all my fault. Mom, can you hear me? Mom?" She took her mother's hand as she lay on the hospital bed.

The monitor beside her started beeping. "What's wrong?" Rebecca asked. Her mother's face was full of alarm.

The doctor came rushing in, a nurse by his side.

"Who are you?" the doctor asked, studying the monitor then adjusting the patient.

"I'm her daughter."

Rebecca let go of her mother's hand so the doctor could get where she was standing. "What's wrong?" Fear covered her face.

"She's in serious pain and not responding to the medication we gave her." The doctor told the nurse something and she rushed out of the room.

"What does that mean?" Rebecca asked.

"I need you to leave for a moment." The doctor turned as the nurse came back with a needle. "Please, ma'am." He looked right at her.

Rebecca took her eyes off her mother and walked out the room, Robert right beside her. She didn't make it two more steps without releasing another gate of tears.

Robert pulled her in his arms for comfort. "I saw a waiting room down the hall." He led her down the corridor, the same way they came, and off to a sitting area. She sat down and he took the chair beside her.

"She's all I have," Rebecca sobbed, choking on tears. "I don't know what I would do without her."

"She's going to be fine."

"You don't know that" Rebecca said, "Why do people always say that when they don't know. I hate those words, I hate 'em, hate 'em, hate 'em." She stomped her feet on the ground in anger.

Robert sat there in silence.

"Oh, Robert." She reached for his hand. "I'm so sorry, I'm glad you're here, really. It's just that…"

"I know, I know."

"I was so horrible to her."

"What?" Robert looked surprise.

"My mom, I was so horrible to her," she repeated. "Growing up, I hated her."

"I'm sure she knew you didn't hate her."

"I did. I told her every day how much I hated her, how much I couldn't wait till I was eighteen to leave. She did everything for me when dad left us. She would do anything for me and I paid her back by hating her, blaming her for the reason I didn't have a father. She never hurt me, even when I did something bad. When she caught me smoking, she said she was disappointed in me but nothing else. She loved me, and I hated her. I hated her so much I left her." Rebecca cried harder. "I told you I lied on the phone."

"Don't worry about it," Robert whispered, thinking of the many lies he'd told.

"No, I want to tell you the truth." She looked him in his eyes. "I ran away from my mom at eighteen, like I said, left her all alone. I thought I knew it all, thought I would run off and have a life. Get a job, no problem. Rent an apartment, no problem. Everything would fall into place. Well, for two years I've been working as a waitress, dancer, anything that would put money in my pocket. What kind of realtor moves for a month because their company tells them to? I'm surprised you bought that."

Robert said nothing.

"Well, I've been here for a month. I work at the bar where I met you. I had just finished my shift and was upset because I couldn't face her. I couldn't face my own mother. I've been trying to find the courage to come back home, admit I was wrong, apologize for everything, tell her I love her, and now it may be too late."

"She knows," Robert said after a few seconds of silence.

"What?"

"She knows you love her," he repeated, looking into her hazel eyes.

"How would you know? The way I treated her, she probably hates me." Rebecca pulled back.

"I want to tell you a story."

Rebecca looked at him.

Robert had never told this story to anyone before, not even Lindsey. It was something he kept to himself.

"My dad took me to the DMV when I was fifteen. I'd just gotten my learner's. I was so excited. My dad beamed with pride when I took my ID photo. We both loved cars. It was something we'd shared since I was a toddler. He would race toy cars around me, making me laugh with the noises he made as sound effects."

Rebecca listened intently.

"I begged him to let me drive home. It was only ten minutes away and after morning rush hour. I begged until he finally gave in. I climbed into our 2000 Honda Civic. My father wanted the best for me and mom, and that was all he could afford. I was so proud driving home, nothing could've stopped me. My dad hid behind nervous smiles the whole way. I was so happy."

Robert started to choke up. "Well…we were two minutes from home at the last stoplight before turning on our road. The light was green. I kept going. An old Ford truck came from the adjacent road— his light was red, but he didn't stop. The police report said the man had been drinking since eight that morning. He smashed right in the passenger side door. The car spun out of control. I was screaming hysterically. I walked away with minor scratches and a broken nose." Robert now had tears streaming down his face. "My dad…"

Rebecca squeezed his hand.

"My dad…"

"It's OK." Rebecca was crying too.

"If I didn't drive or if I didn't have to get my license that day. My dad took off work for me. He was so proud. Maybe if I hadn't…he would still…" Robert took a deep breath.

"It's OK." Rebecca tried to comfort him.

"I need to finish. The day of the funeral, my mom was crying the whole time, from the morning of until late at night. It was late when we returned home. She came up to my room around ten or so and knocked on my door. I too had been crying most the day.

"She sat with me on my bed with something in her hand, an envelope. She gave me a big hug and told me she loved me. That she didn't blame me for what happened and how I shouldn't feel guilty."

Robert held back tears.

"She handed me the note and said my father wanted me to have this if anything happened to him. She hugged me again, kissed me on my forehead, and left the room."

"I remember this as if it were yesterday. I slowly opened the envelope to find a handwritten letter from my dad."

Son,

If you are reading this, I am no longer with you. I don't want you to be upset by my death but blessed you're still alive. Don't mourn me forever, but remember me forever, as a father who loved you very, very much. I tried being the best I could for you and hope and pray that was enough. Take care of your mother. You are the man of the house now. Always stay strong and keep your head held high. Be brave for your mother and yourself. Know that no matter what you do in life, I will always be there in spirit. Keep me close to your heart because you will forever stay in the center of mine. Be safe.

I will forever love you,
Dad

Robert finished, more tears rolling down his face. "I know your mother loves you, no matter what you did."

Rebecca cried even harder.

"Excuse me." The doctor stood in the doorway of the waiting room. "May I speak with you for a minute?" He motioned at Rebecca.

"You can say it here, in front of him." She looked at Robert then back to the man with a troubled look on his face.

"I'm afraid there's no easy way to say this," he began. Rebecca lost control and Robert knew what was coming. The doctor continued. "We tried reviving her, but she was holding on by a thread as it were, I'm sorry." He stood there for a few seconds. "We're going to need you to sign for the body, but please take your time." He looked genuinely sorry.

"No." Rebecca rose quickly, "I'll do it right now."

"Follow me." He directed her to the nurses' station. "She will take care of everything for you. Again, I'm truly sorry for your loss," and with that he walked into the room beside where Rebecca's mother's lifeless body lay.

"Can I see her?" Rebecca asked the nurse.

"Of course you can." The woman behind the counter looked at her with sorrowful eyes. "Would you like to see her before you sign for the body?"

"No, no, I'm right here. I'll go ahead." Rebecca held her hand out for a pen.

"OK, I'm going to need your signature here and here." She marked the spot with X's then handed the pen and clipboard over. "There is one more thing I need you to do."

"Yes."

"I need you to initial and sign below your mother's name. Make sure the spelling's correct please. This is how it will be presented on the death certificate." She marked the spot with her signature and handed the pen back.

Rebecca wrote "Rebecca Downing" right below "Jaime Marie Mason."

"We're going to need to do an autopsy," the nurse added as she took back the clipboard.

"An autopsy?" Rebecca stared through swollen eyes, "Why?"

"Your mother was involved in an ongoing investigation. Didn't you know that?"

"What? No! What crime?"

"Ms. Mason was brought here a few nights ago. She was involved in a hit and run in front of Jefferson Elementary School. The bleeding on the brain caused by the accident, along with her previous medical conditions—I'm amazed that she was able to hold on this long." The nurse turned to check on another patient down the hall.

Robert froze where he stood.

"Oh my…" Rebecca couldn't find the words. She marched in the room where the doctor had gone. "I need a word with you," she said sternly.

"I'm in the middle of something." The doctor looked at her surprised.

"I'll wait outside." Rebecca stormed back to Robert. "Can you believe that?"

He stood there unable to move.

"Robert? Robert?" She waved her hands in front of his face. "Hello?"

"I know." Robert fought to keep his voice from shaking. "What is this world coming to?"

The doctor returned. "Yes?" he asked Rebecca.

"Why didn't you tell me my mother had been in an accident?"

"I thought you knew." The doctor looked taken back. "You didn't know?"

"Does this look like the face of someone who knew?" She was getting louder. "Do the police know who did this?"

"You'd have to ask them." The doctor moved to get away.

"I'm not finished." Rebecca spoke louder. One of the nurses looked up.

"Please keep your voice down. I don't want to have to call security."

"Then answer my questions." She lowered a little. "What detectives?"

"I believe their names were Collins and Jones."

Robert couldn't move an inch.

"Do you have their number?"

"They left their card. It's over by the nurses' station. Now I am deeply sorry for your loss but there are other patients I must tend to." The doctor turned to leave again. Rebecca stopped him once more.

"The nurse mentioned an autopsy?"

"Yes, it's standard for any death during an open investigation."

"When can I get the body?"

"Well…" The doctor thought a moment, but Rebecca cut into his train of thought.

"I want her body back tonight. I'm going to bury her tomorrow," she said without question.

"I'll see what I can do." And with that, he left. This time Rebecca let him go.

She walked over to the counter and tapped her hands quickly to get somebody's attention. "Excuse me." She pounded harder. "Can I get some help?"

"What is it, sweetie?" a young nurse answered with a bright smile.

"Don't *sweetie* me." Rebecca was angry. "I need the number for Detectives Collins and Jones. The doctor said you had it."

The smile disappeared from the nurse as she searched through the contact roller. "Here you go." She wrote down the number on a sticky pad and handed it to her.

Rebecca snatched it without a thank you and made her way towards her mother's room. "Are you coming, Robert? I still need you." She looked at the ghostly white man standing behind her. "Are you all right?"

Robert struggled to speak. "I'm just shocked," he mumbled.

"I know." Rebecca took his wrist. "This must be hard on you because of your father."

"Yeah," Robert agreed. That was the furthest thing from his mind.

"Will you stay with me a little while?"

"Well…" He tried to find an excuse.

"Please." She pulled at him.

He had no choice but to follow.

They walked in. The monitors were turned off and the room was quiet. On the bed lay Jaime Mason, a forty-two-year-old mother who died too young.

"She looks so peaceful," Rebecca whispered.

Robert didn't say anything. He stared at the lifeless body—the woman he'd murdered.

Robert remained with Rebecca for an hour until the coroner came to collect the corpse.

"You'll have her back tomorrow," the gentleman said as he wheeled her off, covering her from view.

Robert and Rebecca made their way down the hall, into the elevators, and out the hospital doors.

"I have to go." Robert spoke first in the parking lot.

"What? You're not coming with me?" Rebecca looked hurt.

"I need to be alone right now," was all he could think to say. "And it might do you some good to do the same. You have a lot to do if there's going to be a funeral tomorrow. With the invitations and the—"

"There aren't going to be any invitations." Rebecca cut him off. "It's just going to be me and I was hoping you would come."

"People need to pay their respects." Robert thought back to his father. "They need to say goodbye."

"I don't know any of her friends. I hadn't talked to her in three years." Rebecca argued.

"It's your mother." Robert stiffened at the words. He had killed somebody's mother. "You do what you think is best."

"I think this is best," Rebecca mumbled more to herself than to Robert. "Will you come, please?"

Every part of Robert's body was screaming no. "I'll see what I can do. I'll call you." He unlocked his car.

"Here, you're going to need my number."

"I already have it. You gave it to me that night."

"I lied about everything—my number too." She pulled out a piece of paper and pen and scribbled down her digits. "Sorry." She thrust the paper into his hands. "Please come."

"I'll call you," Robert said, closing his door. He had to get away—someplace nobody would find him.

He knew just the place.

Chapter 10

Collins took the familiar route back toward the school, past the stop light and stop sign.

"Take a right then go down until Second Street. Take a left, and it's the third house on the right." Jones looked over the map again to make sure of his directional skills. Last thing he wanted was to be in the wrong place with his boss.

Collins followed the directions and pulled in front of a two-story brick house. "Twelve-oh-eight, Second Street?" He looked for conformation from Jones.

"Twelve-oh-eight, Second Street," Andrew echoed.

They got out and shuffled up the pavement to the front door. The house was in a quiet neighborhood, if you didn't count the incident two blocks over. The yard was cut and trimmed with a small bench under the only tree in the front yard.

Collins rang the doorbell.

"Who is it?" a woman's voice penetrated the door.

"Detectives Collins and Jones."

"Hold up your badges, please, to the peephole."

They both held up their badges as asked and waited for a response.

"What's this about?" She didn't open the door.

"Ma'am, could you please open up? It's about your husband." Collins was annoyed at the hostile welcome.

He could hear the chain from the other side fall and the bolt lock turn. The door creaked open.

Standing before him was a petite woman, around five foot. She wore a bright yellow blouse and white loose pants. She had blonde hair to match her shirt and bright blue eyes that looked worried.

"What is it? What's wrong with my husband?" she asked frantically.

"Nothing's wrong with your husband, ma'am," Collins reassured her.

"You said you were here about my husband—what else could it be? What else did those kids do to that man? All he wanted was to help children and this is the thanks he gets." Her words were fast.

"Slow down." Collins laid a hand on her shoulder. "May we come in?"

She hesitated a moment and then agreed. She led them through the hallway filled with pictures of family members and into a formal living room that looked like it hadn't been used in years.

"What's this about?" she asked again as Collins and Jones took a seat on the sofa.

"Why don't you have a seat?" Collins spoke softly.

"Don't tell me to sit in my own home." She walked over and sat down anyways.

"Now, what do you think this is all about, Mrs. Robertson?"

"What else could it be about? Those kids did something else to my husband, didn't they?"

"Why don't you start at the beginning?" He leaned back on the couch relaxed.

"Me and my husband moved out here not too long ago. He was looking for work. He had just gotten laid off. The school was cutting back, something about funding. I just worked at the local dollar store, been there fifteen years. Anyways, he searched for months looking for a position somewhere. I took extra shifts so we could pay the rent and have food."

She leaned back into her chair and then got on the edge, as if nervous about something.

Dave, my husband, had put his application on that Internet job search thing. I don't know what it's called, starts with an M. Monstrous, Mungle..."

"Monster?" Jones came to her rescue.

"That's the one." She pointed a finger at him. "Well, a month or two after he put his application on Monster, he gets a call. The high school down here needs some teachers. We packed up and moved on the spot. Dave got back to teaching. Oh, he loves to teach, loves kids."

"What does he teach?" Collins broke in.

"Chemistry. He's so smart," she continued. "Exams were a week ago and there was these group of kids. Not too smart—didn't try, didn't care, always got pushed up because that No Child Left Behind thing the government did. Dumbest thing they ever came up with, if you ask me. If the child ain't smart enough, don't push 'em to the next grade."

"Anyways, these group of kids, they didn't pass the class. Must have been about five or six of them. Dave felt so bad for them, but he don't just give grades out. You got to earn them, that's what he always said. He tried tutoring after school, hoping they would show up, but they never did."

Collins took in a deep breath but said nothing.

"Exams came and those kids failed—first "F" Dave ever wrote on them report cards. A couple days afterwards, he drove to work like always. When he came out, the front end of his car was torn up. The school looked back on those video cameras they have everywhere at that high school. Sure enough, it was the same five or six kids breaking the headlight with a baseball bat."

"They were all going to be suspended but Dave wouldn't let the school board do that. He dropped the charges, said if they got expelled they would never catch up. Then they would be just another child slipped through the system's cracks."

"Where is your husband now?" Collins looked at his watch. "It's after four on a Saturday."

"I told you, he does tutoring for kids who want or need the extra help, every day except Sunday. He'd do anything for those children." She smiled at the thought.

"You said the kids only hit the front of his car?" Collins rubbed his chin. "Why not the rest of the vehicle?"

"They only had one bat and five kids. They each wanted a turn. My guess, each was going to start at the front and work their way back. The next one would make sure nothing got missed. Only three of them were able to take a swing before one of the faculty members saw what was happening and yelled from the window. They took off, five guys and only one bat." She shook her head. "Told you they weren't too bright."

"Why did your husband come home so late last Wednesday?"

"Field trip to Washington D.C. Dave was a chaperone. Didn't get back till late."

"Thank you for your time, Mrs. Robertson." Collins got up to leave. Jones followed.

"Wait a minute. I answered your questions, what about mine?" She chased after them.

"We are investigating the hit and run two blocks over, and with the frontal damage to your husband's SUV, you can put two and two together and see why we thought of him." Collins stood at the front door.

Mrs. Robertson stopped in her tracks. "How dare you! This whole neighborhood, this whole town...always accusing the new people of everything."

"Thanks for your time, Mrs. Robertson." And with that, Collins and Jones walked out, leaving the door open.

"Why doesn't she trust anybody?" Jones asked as he opened the passenger side door.

"My guess is she had a rough childhood—drunken dad, pill popping mom. Dave the schoolteacher loved her, something she'd never felt before. Although she trusts him, she finds it hard to trust anybody else." Collins started the engine.

"How do you get that, from *that*?" Andrew looked over his shoulder in the direction of Mrs. Robertson's closed door.

"Seen it before." Collins ended the conversation. "When we get back, go over those license plates again. I want every single ID of anyone passing through that stoplight this time."

"Yes, sir," Jones replied.

Robert drove down the familiar country road near his empty oasis. The two-story country destination was waiting for him when he pulled up the graveled driveway. This was his only place of solitude in the world.

He slid out the car and went up the porch, skipping the broken step. There was plenty of sunlight beaming through the windows and he had no problem making it up the stairs and into his favorite room.

The lantern was turned over by the wall. No light emitted from behind the glass. Robert leaned over to pick it up. He remembered abandoning this item, and although it was hopeless, he hit the power button, hoping once more, the light would shine bright for him again. Nothing happened. He threw it against the wall in a sudden burst of anger. The glass shattered over the floor.

He screamed out, pounding the walls, punching holes in the sheetrock he'd worked so hard to put up. He fell over on to the floor and leaned up against the wall. Everything in his life was going wrong. He looked up to the ceiling, tears streaming down his face. "God, please fix this," he prayed as he rested his head against the part of the wall still intact.

Robert closed his eyes and tried to push everything from his mind. He was physically and mentally exhausted and soon fell asleep.

"Push!" the nurse yelled as Lindsey screamed in pain. "Come on, push!"

"You almost got it, baby," Robert coached alongside her.

"I see something," the obstetrician said with excitement. "OK, the head is clear. Now on the count of three, I'm going to need you to push as hard as you possibly can. One..."

"Two," Robert took over. "Three! Push, baby, push." He was bursting with excitement and anxiety. He was about to become a father and didn't know if he was ready for this.

"It's a boy," the doctor beamed as he wiped the fluid from the nose and mouth. He handed the newborn to one of the nurses to clean up.

"Did you hear that, honey? We have a boy. We have a son. My son." Robert felt light headed. Lindsey cried from joy and the pain of childbirth.

"Here you go." The nurse came over, holding the baby in a blue blanket. She handed him to Lindsey. "What's his name?"

"Joshua. Joshua Tyler Armes." She leaned in to kiss her infant's forehead.

"That's a beautiful name." The nurse smiled while writing it on the birth certificate.

"Hi, baby, I'm your mama." Lindsey beamed over her little bundle of joy.

"And I'm your daddy." Robert nestled in close to both of them. *"And we both love you so very, very much. I can't believe this."* He leaned in to kiss Lindsey on the lips. *"Our little miracle is finally here."*

"Can you believe it? We're parents."

Robert flashed back to his own parents—his mom had just passed away a year before he was married. A stroke. His dad had been in the car accident.

"I wish my parents had lived to see this."

"I know, honey. I'm sure they would be proud of you. I know I am."

"Dad would be thrilled we named the baby after him." Robert smiled at baby Joshua, who was looking up at him with big eyes.

"It felt right."

"We did it, babe. We did it."

"I know, honey. He's beautiful." A tear rolled down her face. *"I love you, Robert."*

"I love you too, Lindsey."

Robert woke suddenly, his phone was ringing.

"Hello?" he answered, yawning.

"Where are you? I've been trying to reach you for hours." Lindsey's voice was loud and clear on the other end.

"I'm finishing up here at the office," Robert lied. "Those papers took longer than I thought. I'm on my way now. I should be there in twenty minutes."

Lindsey hung up on him.

Great, he thought as he pulled himself to his feet. *I wonder what I did wrong this time.*

He hobbled down the steps and out the door, skipping the broken step. He hopped in the Envoy and sped off down the country road.

The sun was beginning to fall from the sky. So peaceful.

He pulled down the street and into the drive and slowly got out the car. A shiver crossed over him as he walked up the sidewalk. It was sixty-five degrees outside.

"Where have you been?" Lindsey screamed before he barely made it through the front door.

"I told you I was at work." He matched her volume.

"Work? Work! I've called your work ten times today. Every time, you were nowhere to be found. Care to explain?"

Robert stalled, trying to think of something. "I was with Jimmy today. I needed a break after that huge sale. We went to the golf course. He had a membership coupon thing so I could play for free, happy? Now calm down."

"Calm down? Calm down? You want me to calm down!" Lindsey stormed into the kitchen.

"Sorry, I lied this morning about maybe finding work."

An unsettling silence passed over them.

"So you were with Jimmy today?"

"Yep," Robert replied calmly.

"All day?"

"Yep, all day. Except when I went to the office to file those papers."

"So if I called Jimmy, he would back your story?" She looked him dead in the eye.

"Do you want the number?"

"I can't believe this!"

"What?"

"Are you cheating on me?" Lindsey changed the subject quickly.

"What are you talking about?" Robert asked confused.

"Are you cheating on me?"

"No." Robert stood his ground. "What would make you think that?"

"Who were you talking to this morning?" Lindsey changed the subject again.

"What?"

"This morning." Lindsey used the counter to steady herself. "Who was on the phone?"

"I told you." Robert tried to sound convincing, "Jimmy."

"If I called Jimmy right now, right this very second, he would tell me he called you this morning?"

"What do you want me to say?" Robert yelled

"The truth!" Lindsey screamed.

"I just told you—"

"Liar!" Lindsey cut into his words with such pain in her voice. "I called Jimmy's wife today to ask her if she would take me to the store, since you had the car."

Robert could see where this was going.

"She did, and on the way to the market, I thanked her for the lift. I asked her to thank Jimmy on my behalf for helping you with work in construction. You can imagine how that conversation went?" Lindsey didn't stop for an answer. "She didn't know what I was talking about, so I let it go. When I returned home, I debated for an hour whether to phone Jimmy and ask him myself, or just let it be and trust my husband. You can see which side of me won. I called him. He didn't know what I was talking about, said he hadn't talked with you in days. He was going to call tomorrow and see if everything was OK. So Robert," Lindsey took a deep breath, "where the hell were you today, and don't you dare lie to me."

"Another friend of mine wanted me to help him with something."

"What friend?"

"Tony."

"What's Tony's number?"

"I don't—"

"You don't what Robert? You don't have it? Is that what you were going to say? Does Tony live in the dark ages, still using carrier pigeons to send messages? Maybe he's deaf and he can't use a phone? Is that what you were going to say?"

Robert didn't bother to defend himself.

141

"Are you cheating on me?" Lindsey asked, exhausted.

"No."

"Get out."

"What?"

"Get out now!"

"Lindsey, I wasn't cheating on you."

"Get out!"

"Lindsey."

"Just go!" She picked up one of her worn out cook books and threw it at him. "I packed you a suitcase full of clothes, now go." Tears were slowly falling down her face.

Robert didn't say another word and picked up the suitcase. "I love you," he said, but even those words sounded strange to him.

Lindsey slammed the door behind him. He could hear her crying from the other side.

Robert slowly walked down the steps he had just come up and again got back into his car. He sat there staring at the apartment complex, wondering if he should go back in.

He decided not to and started the engine, heading back to the countryside.

That house would finally be used tonight.

Jones slammed his keyboard down in frustration. "There's nothing here suspecting any of these people of the hit and run. No body shop within a hundred miles has any of these cars in their garage."

Collins walked around Jones' desk to look at the computer screen. "We'll have to take them one by one like we planned until one pans out. Get hard copies of all the names and addresses."

Jones quickly printed and matched the addresses with each owner. "Here you go, boss." He stood at Collins' desk with a small stack of papers held out.

"Why are there only eight names here? Nine cars passed through the light, not counting the one we followed up on today."

"One didn't have a name, just an address. A car rental place." Jones pointed out the last page in Collins' hand.

"And you called the shop?"

"I did this morning. No car was reported matching the description of the vehicle."

"Did you ask if anyone rented a car in the past three days?" Collins stood up from his desk.

"No. Should I?" Jones stepped back out of fear.

"Would I have asked if I didn't think it was important?" Collins moved from behind his desk. "What time do they close?"

"Around five, sir." Jones looked confused.

Collins glanced at his wristwatch then took a deep breath. It was six thirty. "What time do they open?"

"Tomorrow's Sunday." Jones racked his brain for an answer. "Around two."

"Be there at two tomorrow, not a minute later." Collins turned to leave.

"What about the rest of the suspects?"

"We will start with the one at the dealership tomorrow." Collins was at the door. "Go home, be with your wife in your new home. Make a memory or two." Collins walked out the door and into the evening air.

The sun was starting to fall past the horizon as he sped out the parking lot.

Chapter 11

Robert pulled back up the graveled driveway of the old country home, like many of times before. Only this time he knew he would be staying the whole night. He put the car in park and grabbed the bulging suitcase beside him. He dragged his feet through the grass and up the porch, skipping the broken step like always, and walked past the front door.

The sun had disappeared from the sky.

"Why didn't I get a flashlight?" he mumbled as he climbed the stairwell to the room that would never be finished.

Robert didn't know why he chose this room to sleep in. The walls were barely hanging on and there was little insulation. There were better places to sleep in this empty home. The bathtub would have been perfect because Lindsey didn't pack a blanket or pillow for him and there was no bed.

He stayed in the room.

Robert opened the suitcase. Lying on top of everything was Lindsey's wedding ring. He hadn't noticed she wasn't wearing it when they were arguing. He reached for his around his finger and noticed too he hadn't put his back on when he left the hospital. Tears started to form around the edges of his eyes. Underneath the circle bond between man and wife lay a torn sheet of paper with hasty writing. Only one line had been written.

Maybe when you're honest with me, we can work this out.

Robert clenched Lindsey's ring so tight his knuckles turned white and his fingernails made an impression on the inside of his palm.

He pulled out some clothes and placed them on the wooden floor to lie on. Then he reached for a couple of sweaters, one with his name on it. Lindsey had made it for his birthday about eight months ago. They couldn't afford to buy anything new. He rested his head on the duffel bag.

He rolled onto his back, holding the wedding band to his face, turning it over in his hands. The note close to his chest as he breathed softly, unsteady. Slowly, he drifted to sleep. He never let go of that ring.

"Great news, honey," Robert said as he walked through the front door of his country home, carrying a bag full of groceries.

"What?" Lindsey questioned as she dangled a set of plastic colored keys in front of Joshua, who was laughing and grasping for the assortments of colors on the floor in the living room.

"I lost my job."

"What!"

"I got fired today."

Robert put the bags on the counter and made his way to his wife and son, completely oblivious to the stare from Lindsey.

"What does this mean for us financially?" Lindsey asked, trying to keep her voice low as not to upset her giggling toddler.

"We're fine," Robert replied, trying hard to keep a straight face.

"What are we going to do? We don't have any money saved up. We were barely making it as it was."

"I don't know," Robert said too enthusiastically.

Lindsey picked Joshua up from the floor and held him tight. A worried expression covered her face. "What is so funny?"

"I got a new job."

"What? Already?"

"Yep. A better job with more benefits and health care—the works." Robert was smiling from ear to ear.

"What are you talking about? How did this happen?"

"Our company was bought out today," Robert began. "Our entire real estate building and associates were completely taken over by a bigger corporation from up north." Robert got up and made his way back into the kitchen.

"I don't understand." Lindsey jumped up and followed. Her bundle of joy was resting in her arms.

Robert reached into the bags and pulled out a couple of T-bone steaks. "We are going to eat like royalty tonight."

"We can't afford this," Lindsey exclaimed, staring at the red meat, which cost a week's worth of baby food. "What happened to everyone at the company?"

"Some were transferred, others are going to stay."

"Stay?"

"With the bigger company."

"Robert, if you don't tell me what is going on right now, I'm going to—"

"I got promoted."

"What?"

"I'm going to be the manager for their corporation in this region. The company that bought out our agency told me today. They were so impressed at my sales records over the past year and half, they offered me the job. Said I knew the neighborhood better than anyone here, and they want me to run the branch. Can you believe that?"

"What!" Lindsey squealed softly, trying not to wake Joshua, who was now fast asleep.

"I received a promotion, a pay raise, benefit package, 401K, and health care for the whole family."

"Oh, Robert," Lindsey said, all smiles. "See, I knew everything would turn around after you sold that house to the detective and his wife. What were their names again?"

"I don't even remember, it's been so long ago."

"Hello?" Collins picked up the phone. He was driving down the interstate, ready to pull off onto an exit he only took once a year.

"Detective Collins?" A woman's voice was on the other end.

"Who is this? How did you get my number?" he asked as he put on his turn signal.

"My name is Rebecca Downing. My mother is Jaime Mason, I believe you are investigating her murder."

"Your mother, she's dead?" Collins asked surprised at the new information.

"Yes, you didn't know? She died this afternoon."

Those doctors, Collins thought angrily. I told them to call if anything happened, what's wrong with people?

"Detective?"

"I'm sorry to hear that. You have my deepest sympathy." Collins drove down a deserted road.

"I don't want your sympathy, Detective. I want the person responsible brought to justice."

"You and me both." Collins neared his destination. "Was there anything else?" he asked as he scanned the road.

"I wanted to know if you had any leads."

"I can't discuss an open investigation to the public."

"The public? I'm not the public, I'm her daughter."

"That may be," Collins was getting agitated, he hated these phone calls, "but I can't speak to anyone about the case, not until it's been closed."

There was a brief silence.

"OK, I understand."

"Have a good night," Collins said out of courtesy.

"Wait!"

"Yes?"

"I'm having a funeral tomorrow for my mother, and well…if you and your partner would like to come, I would really appreciate it.

I'm sure my mother would too. Especially because you are the men trying to bring her peace in death and her killer to justice."

"I'll see what I can do." Collins hung up the phone. He made a point never to talk to the family members involved in a case, especially when the case was a homicide.

Collins reached his destination. He pulled into a silent cemetery, now completely dark. He drove about twenty feet before stopping. Collins slowly turned the engine off, leaving on the headlights.

An owl hooted somewhere off in the background as he opened his door and stepped out into the desolate night, a handful of blue flowers in his right hand.

Roughly ten feet away rested a lonely tombstone, kept cut by the grounds caretaker. A decayed flower stem rested against a small rock.

"Quiet night," Collins spoke to the empty graveyard, "How you've been?" he looked right at the headstone. "I've been good," he answered as if someone spoke to him. "I've been working hard on a case. I think I've almost figured it out," he trailed off. "I can't believe it's been nearly thirty years. How are mom and dad? I've really missed you, all of you. Sometimes I feel so alone. Becky left me." He stopped. "I know, I know. She said I put my career in front of her—can you believe it?" Collins stifled a soft tear. "Well, I just came by to say hello, I miss ya. You were the only one who was always there for me. I love you." Collins leaned down to replace the dead flowers with the newer ones. "I'll see you later." He walked slowly back to his car and drove off into the night.

BELOVED SON AND BROTHER, 1954 – 1980 was written on the tombstone, surrounded by the men and women fallen during battle.

Robert woke to the sunshine streaming down on his face, his wife's ring still in his hand as he moved to get up.

"Ugh," he moaned, struggling to move after sleeping on the wood floor all night. His phone rang.

"Lindsey?" he answered without looking at the caller ID.

"Rebecca," the voice on the other end corrected him. "Who's Lindsey?"

"My sister," Robert lied, as he rubbed his forehead. "What do you want?"

"I was calling to see if you wanted me to pick you up or if you wanted to meet at the funeral."

"I don't think I'm coming." Robert searched for a valid excuse. "I have a meeting today."

"On Sunday?"

Robert didn't know what day of the week it was. He didn't know what month it was. "I thought today was Monday," he said lamely.

"So do you want me to pick you up or are you going to meet me at the funeral?" Rebecca repeated. "I really need somebody there with me."

Robert moaned, "I'll meet you there."

"Thanks," she said softly, "it's the cemetery right off Route 15. You know where's that's at?"

"I know," Robert mumbled.

"At one thirty."

"OK." Robert hung up the phone.

How could he go? Thoughts were racing through his head. *This is the woman I killed. I can't go to her funeral, even if it was an accident. Who's going to believe me? I've waited this long and told nobody, it's too late now.*

Robert looked at the time. It was already ten thirty. Only three hours away. *Maybe this will all be buried with the coffin. Maybe it'll all go away with her.* He convinced himself of this as he searched through his bag to find a dress shirt, tie, and pants, surprised to see them rolled up at the bottom.

Collins pulled up to the graveyard, dressed in a black suit and black tie. Jones wasn't with him. He had decided not to tell him. Collins wasn't sure himself if he was going until two hours ago. He had no need to. He didn't know the woman, he didn't know the family, and he didn't know anybody here, but something inside him told him to come.

Collins spotted the coffin perched up on the same steel rods that would be lowering it into the ground in about fifteen minutes. He looked at his watch. It was one thirty, time for the burial process to begin. He strutted up the small hill and stood behind the blue chairs arranged for family and close friends of the deceased. He noticed there was an unusually small crowd. In the front, he spotted the back of a woman with red hair he assumed to be Rebecca—beside her a man. *Maybe her husband,* he thought. Behind another row of chairs were about seven people sitting here and there, waiting for the funeral to begin.

"We are gathered on this somber occasion," the preacher spoke, "to bury a loved one, a mother, a friend, someone who will stay in a special place in our hearts. We pray God lifts her spirit up to Him. We can take comfort in the fact she is walking with the Lord and her pain and sorrows are no more."

The woman in the front row began to cry.

"We say our final goodbyes to the woman we knew, knowing one day we will meet again. Let us pray."

Collins bowed his head and said, "Amen" out of respect. He waited as people walked to the casket to say farewell. Rebecca was the first to go. Collins watched as she placed a hand on the coffin, crying softly, and holding on to her husband. She moved on and other mourners followed.

"I am so sorry for your loss." Collins caught Rebecca's eye as she walked by.

"Thank you." She held out a hand to shake his. "How did you know my mother?"

"I'm Detective Collins, ma'am. We spoke on the phone last night." He noticed the man following her stiffen. All the color drained from his face.

"Oh, right, nice to finally meet you. Thank you so much for coming." She paused a moment, "Do you have any news?"

"As I told you last night, I can't discuss a case, but we are following a lead."

The man beside her flinched.

"Oh." Her eyes lit up. "When will you know anything?"

"I can't be too sure. Just have to follow the clues and see where they take us."

"Did you hear, Robert?" She turned toward the man beside her.

"Yeah," Robert answered softly, "that's great."

"Hello." Collins extended his hand toward Robert, "I'm Detective Phil Collins."

"Robert Armes." Robert grasped Collins hand, but he didn't make eye contact. "I'm sorry about your...mother-in-law?"

"Oh, no," Rebecca chimed in with a weak smile. "Robert's just a..." she looked at him, "just a good friend. If it wasn't for him, I don't know how I would have been able to make it through this tough time."

"Nice to meet you." Collins nodded his head, but Robert still didn't look at him. "I know what it's like to lose a family member."

"I'm sorry." Rebecca looked like she was about to cry again. "Does it get easier?"

"The pain never really goes away."

"Excuse me." A young woman broke in the conversation. She didn't look older than twenty-five.

"Yes?" Rebecca asked, startled by the new face.

"Can I have a minute of your time?"

"I have to get going." Collins moved to leave. "Again sorry for your loss."

"Please keep in touch. Let me know if you find anything," Rebecca called after him.

Collins didn't answer. Instead, he looked at the ghost white man standing by the deceased's daughter. *That's strange*, he thought as he unlocked his car, got in, and drove off, ready to see if his lead would indeed pan out.

He picked up his cell phone and called Jones. "Meet me at the shop in twenty minutes." He didn't wait for a response before hanging up. He had a good feeling about his next stop.

Robert arrived at the funeral, already sweating. *I shouldn't be here.* The thought kept racing through his mind as his legs, without thinking, automatically walked toward the burial site.

Rebecca spotted him and grabbed him by the arm. "Thanks for coming."

Robert let her lead him to the front row, in front of the wooden coffin. *The lady I killed is right there.* His head was splitting. *I shouldn't be here.*

The preacher began but Robert didn't hear a word except the pounding in his heart, echoing into his ears.

Rebecca moved to get up, reaching for his hand as she did. Robert came back from his unconscious-like state as he was dragged to the casket. *I shouldn't be here. I'm so sorry.* His thoughts were swirling. *I'm sorry, please forgive me.* He didn't reach to touch the wooden box but imagined the woman lying underneath two inches of wood.

He allowed himself to be taken away by Rebecca pulling at him.

A man's voice echoed distantly around his brain when Rebecca stopped to talk to someone. *I need to get away*, he kept thinking. *I need to run.*

A jolt of awareness coursed through his body when the word "detective" was spoken from the man's mouth.

He flinched a second later at the sound of a lead, then zoned out. *Does he know?* Robert was getting dizzy. He has to know. *Why else would he be here if there was a lead to follow up on? Why hasn't he arrested me? Should I flee?*

Just as Robert was about to bolt, the detective was gone and replaced by a younger woman around Rebecca's age.

Robert felt Rebecca's hand slip into his as she dragged him away yet again to a nearby bench, out of ear range of the funeral congregation.

"I would like to speak to you alone," he heard the woman say.

"It's all right, anything you need to say can be said in front of him."

"That's fine." Robert saw this as his chance to flee. "I'll be over there." He pointed at his car.

"No!" Rebecca held tight to his arm.

"It's OK, I don't mind." Robert released her grip and tried desperately to get away.

"No. I need you here." She pulled him down beside her.

Robert was trapped.

"What did you want?" Rebecca asked the woman.

"I don't know where to begin."

"How about your name?"

"Right, my name," the woman echoed Rebecca's words. "My name is Tiffany Mouser."

"How did you know my mother?" Rebecca pushed the process along.

Tiffany hesitated. "She gave me a kidney."

Rebecca almost fell off the bench. Robert too was wondering if he'd heard right. Rebecca found her balance and asked, astounded, making sure she had heard correctly. "A kidney?"

"Yes." Tiffany lifted her dress shirt to reveal a scar.

"Why would my mother do that?"

"She was dying and so was I."

"Excuse me," Rebecca stared at her, "you were dying?"

"Yes." Tiffany looked into her eyes. "My kidneys haven't functioned well since I was a little girl. I had one transplant around ten or so and I needed another. The first one was failing. A condition passed down by my mother."

"Where is your mother? Why didn't she give you a transplant?"

"My mother died giving birth to me."

Rebecca reached out for her hand. "I'm so sorry."

"That's OK, you didn't know."

"What does this have to do with my mother's death?"

"Like I said, she was dying and I was dying. She had an abnormal heart murmur. The doctors said it wasn't looking good for her..."

"Why did she give away one of her kidneys?" Rebecca cut in. "Why didn't she wait until she died, for a transplant? She could have used that kidney to get well."

"I was given two more months to live and your mother wanted me to have one of hers before it was too late. We didn't know if my body would accept her organ, or if the process would work. If it didn't, I could try again with her other kidney, assuming I lived longer than Jaime."

"What about your father? Where was he? Why didn't he give you a kidney?"

"My father died at war before I was born. He met my mom while on an army base in Texas. She got pregnant. He didn't know until after he was shipped out. They were going to marry when he returned, but he never did." She took a deep breath. "I've been an orphan all my life. I wanted to see where I came from, where my father grew up.

"That doesn't explain how you met my mother?"

"I had a bad incident about four months ago. I was taken to Lakeside Memorial Hospital where I found out I needed the transplant. That's when I first met your mother. She was there for a checkup. She passed by my room on her way out and saw I was in pain. There weren't any doctors or nurses in the room. She came in and made sure I was tended to."

Robert sat still as a statue beside Rebecca, listening intently. The detective had escaped his mind for a moment.

"She stayed with me that night, in the hospital. She prayed with me and taught me about God. I was released the next day, Sunday. She took me with her to church."

Rebecca stared, eyes wide.

"I was out of money. I had found the place where my father used to live before he passed away. I didn't have the courage to walk up to the front door. I stood outside for two days staring at the house until a man came by and asked me to leave. I didn't have anywhere to go. Your mother took me into her home, gave me food, fresh clothes, and a bed to sleep in. I believe it was your old room."

Rebecca started to tear up again.

"I would go with her to the hospital for her checkups, and she would go with me to mine. For the first time in my life, I felt like I had a mother. She would talk all the time about a daughter she had around my age. Told me she ran off at eighteen and how it broke her heart. She always wished you would come back. Jaime wanted to tell you how much she loved you. She wasn't mad about what happened between the two of you."

Rebecca shifted a little on the bench.

"During the last few weeks, her condition was getting worse. She was fighting an infection along the transplant's incision. She drew up a will and had me sign as a witness. She left everything to you."

159

Tears were now streaming down Rebecca's face.

"She asked me to find you, like I had found my dad's place. I promised her I would, no matter how long it took."

"The night of the accident, we were both doing a fundraiser at Jefferson Elementary School. We were hosting a twenty-four-hour charity event to raise money for women's health. The school was on break for a week. Jaime had already been there twelve hours. I took over and forced her to go home. She wanted to stay, but I told her it wasn't a good idea with her condition. She reluctantly agreed to leave for a few hours and get some sleep. That's when it happened." Tiffany burst into tears. "If I hadn't made her go or if I let her stay just two more minutes."

"It's not your fault." Rebecca reached over and embraced Tiffany. "There was no way you could have known. There was nothing you could have done." Rebecca hugged her tighter.

"I'm so sorry." Tiffany cried into her shirt.

"The only person who is at fault is whoever did this to my mother." Rebecca pulled back to look at Tiffany's sorrowful face.

Across the field, Jaime Mason was being lowered into the ground.

"How did you know about the funeral?"

"I went to the hospital before church this morning to see her. The nurse told me what happened. When I asked her why she didn't call me, she said her daughter claimed the body. She overheard you telling the doctor about the funeral, how you wanted it today. I knew where she wanted to be buried. I told everyone at church and then came here."

"The police are going to find the person responsible for this."

"I'm so sorry," was all Tiffany was able to get out during sobs.

Robert sat on the bench, beside the two crying women, until they both stood and decided it was finally time to go.

Chapter 12

Jones was leaning against his sedan when Collins pulled into the rental shop and parked.

"What are you waiting for?" Collins asked getting out.

"I was waiting for you."

"Have you talked to anyone yet?"

Collins made his way toward the door.

"I didn't know if you wanted me to."

"We are trying to solve a homicide, Jones. Some things you can't wait for."

A salesman immediately met them as they walked in. "Hello, gentlemen, is there something I can help you with?"

Collins reached for his badge. "I'm Detective Collins and this is Detective Jones. We need to speak to a manager immediately."

The man looked shocked. "Yes, sir." He quickly rushed off toward the back, only to return a few seconds later with a taller man in a suit.

"Hi, I'm Earl Snyder. Is there something I can help you with?"

"I need to know if any cars were returned here with frontal damage within the past five days."

"I already called and talked with a manager," Jones jumped in, trying to defend himself against the negligence Collins was inadvertently implying.

Collins glared at him. "Don't interrupt me." He spun back around to face the manager. "Well?"

163

"As your partner stated," he nodded toward, Jones who had shrunk back a couple feet, "we haven't."

"Look, I know how these places work."

"Excuse me," the manager looked taken back.

"The SUV we are looking for only has frontal damage—a broken headlight, maybe a couple dents. Now I know you would have a very hard time renting or selling a recently abused vehicle. Maybe, just maybe, when this car was sent away to be worked on, the papers didn't get logged for whatever reason. Therefore, any documents pertaining to the car in the future would be nonexistent, ensuring it could be sold for face value without anyone knowing that very same SUV was involved in an accident—a homicide." Collins was now red-faced from the ignorance of the man standing before him.

"That's a pretty big accusation." The manager looked almost frightened but held his ground. "I hope you have some proof to back your story."

"I could go get a warrant," Collins started, "but that would take a day, maybe two depending on the situation. I could get one to search this entire warehouse and every storage facility owned by the company. I'm sure one little car isn't worth what may or may not be found while searching the compounds thoroughly, and I do mean stripping down every wall until I find what I'm looking for. Am I getting through to you?" Collins looked the man straight in the eye.

"Let me see what I can find." The manager scurried off to the safety of his office.

164

"Sir, can you really do that?" Jones asked, almost afraid to speak.

"It doesn't matter if I can. I need him to think I can."

"What if the SUV isn't here?"

"Oh, it's here," Collins assured himself.

"Even so, we would still need a warrant for the rental information."

"Fear is a funny thing," was all Collins said as he turned around to face the doorway the manager disappeared behind.

Robert jumped into his Envoy the second he was free from Rebecca and sped off toward the apartment. He had to make sure Lindsey wasn't linked to him, to any of this. The detectives would figure it out before too much longer. He needed to get a couple of things and leave before it was too late.

"Open up, Lindsey," Robert hollered through the door.

"Go away," she yelled back at him. "I thought you would get the message. I need space."

"Lindsey, open up, I have to tell you something and then I'm gone." Robert pleaded through the door, looking over his shoulders as a car passed by. "Please!"

"Why should I believe you? All you've done is lie to me."

"Whatever you want to know, I'll tell you. Please open the door."

"I'm going to call the police if you aren't gone in five minutes."

"I promise I'll leave if you let me in," Robert begged, banging on the door.

"Why don't you disappear for a couple of days and come back? Maybe I'll let you in then."

"I wanted to give you your ring back." Robert was trying anything to get past the inches of wood that separated them. "I'm ready to start over."

"We need more time."

"I don't have time."

"What?" Lindsey's voice lowered in confusion and surprise.

"The police are after me." Robert gave up on lying and decided to tell the truth for once.

"What?"

"The police are after me, I did something terrible. Please let me in." Robert pounded harder on the door. His hand was going numb.

"What did you do?"

"Let me in and I'll explain everything, I promise," he pleaded—his last attempt.

To his surprise, he heard the bolts unlock and the door open.

"What's going on?" Lindsey asked, her eyes opened wide in wonderment but not fear.

"I did something horrible several nights ago."

Robert pushed open the door and slammed it behind him. He rushed toward the bedroom. Lindsey chased after him.

"What did you do? Cheat the government out some money at your job? Outstanding parking tickets? Traffic violations? What's so terrible?"

"I killed somebody!" Robert yelled, tired of keeping it all inside.

Lindsey fell over backwards onto the dresser. "What!"

"It was an accident. I was driving home from Rebecca's hotel."

"Rebecca?"

Robert continued as if he didn't hear her. "I was still buzzed from the drinks I had that night, and there was something going on at the elementary school. I didn't see the woman walk out onto the street. I didn't stop at the stop sign. I didn't know what to do."

"You were the hit and run in front of the school?"

Lindsey backed into the kitchen.

"It was an accident. I didn't mean to hurt her. I didn't know what to do. I had alcohol on my breath. I rolled through a stop sign. I didn't see her. It was dark out."

"Why didn't you stay? Why didn't you help her? Why didn't you turn yourself in?"

"There was no way I could have. I didn't want to go to prison; the alcohol alone would put me away for years. I thought I covered my tracks. I thought I was careful. It was an accident. I called the police and waited until I was sure she was OK. I thought she would be OK. It was an accident." Robert pulled everything out of the closet.

"Rebecca—who is she, your accomplice?" Lindsey was slowly making her way to the phone.

"She's this girl I met at a bar. I was so angry with you, with us, I screwed up." Robert was throwing everything he owned, everything he needed into a suitcase.

"You screwed up? You screwed up!" Lindsey picked up the phone. "I'm calling the police."

"No!" Robert jumped and tackled her onto the sofa. "Wait, wait!"

"Help! Help!" Lindsey hollered at the top of her lungs.

Robert covered her mouth with his hands. "Wait a second, just wait a second," he begged.

Lindsey bit at his fingers to get free. "Help! Help!"

Robert ran back to the bedroom and grabbed the half-opened suitcase on the bed and ran for the door. "I'm so sorry, baby." He stopped and turned to face her, the phone in her hand.

"Nine-one-one, what's your emergency?"

Lindsey stared at her husband.

Robert took this chance to finish what he needed to say. "I came here to tell you everything so the police couldn't blame anything on you. Accomplice, aiding and abetting—I didn't want to bring you down with me."

Lindsey didn't move.

"Hello? Anybody there?" The 911 operator's voice rang out during the awkward silence between the couple.

Robert didn't waste any more time, "I love you," he yelled as he leaped out the front door to the curious eyes of the neighbors coming to see the commotion.

Robert jumped into the Envoy and drove out the driveway for the last time.

Collins waited patiently until the manger returned to the showroom.

"Apparently, there was a 2007 Honda Pilot turned in several days ago. It wasn't logged in the books. Unfortunately, all the repairs are done and the vehicle is being shipped back to this building as we speak."

Collins tried to remain calm. "What did you do with the tires?"

"Excuse me?"

"The tires," Collins repeated, "on the Honda—what did you do with them?"

"They are still on the car, I suppose, unless they were damaged in the crash."

"For your sake, you'd better hope not."

"Sir?" Jones called from the corner. "I've just received a 911 dispatch I think we should take."

"Why is that?" Collins asked, not taking his eyes off Earl.

"Because the woman who called said her husband was involved with the hit and run in front of Jefferson Elementary School."

Collins turned on Jones, "what?"

"That's what the dispatcher said."

"Come on!" Collins yelled as he took off running toward his car.

Collins drove with blue lights flashing as fast he could toward the address given by the dispatcher at the station. "We've got 'em now." Collins swerved in and out of traffic in a race to get to the scene.

Jones sat anxiously in the passenger seat.

When they arrived, the place was already swarming with local PD and concerned neighbors.

Collins parked on the curb and got out, already reaching for his badge. "I'm Detective Collins. This is Detective Jones," he spoke to a man standing guard. "What happened here?"

"As far as I can tell, it's a domestic disturbance."

"What about the part where the woman said her husband was involved with vehicular manslaughter?"

"Women will say anything to attract the police when there is an abusive spouse." He turned to spit some dip on the ground.

"Abusive? What makes you so sure?"

"Look at this place," he eyed the neighborhood, "and wait till you get inside. Has domestic aggression written all over it."

Collins walked through the front door. The guard wasn't kidding. The place was a wreck. The molding around the ceiling was cracked. There were small dents in the wall and some of the furniture looked like it had been moved involuntarily.

"Hello." Collins introduced himself to a woman on the sofa. "I'm Detective Collins. I'll take it from here." He relieved the officer sitting beside the brunette. "Can you tell me your name, please?"

"I already gave all my information to that man over there." She pointed toward an officer in the corner.

"That may be, but I have a few questions of my own I would like to ask, if that's OK with you."

"What do you want to know?"

"Your name"

"My name is Lindsey Armes. It's going to be Lindsey Myers when I get a divorce from my murderous husband."

"Who is your husband?"

Collins pulled out a pad and began to write.

"Robert Armes." She crinkled her nose.

"And why do you think Mr. Armes is a murderer?"

"Because he killed some woman."

"He told you this?"

"Yes, yes, he told me." Lindsey nodded. "Then he packed all his clothes and ran out."

"Do you know where he might have gone?"

"No, how could I?" Lindsey asked, offended.

"A place he may have mentioned in the past?"

"The only other place he went was to the office, and he tried to stay there as much as possible." Lindsey shivered.

"Do you know why that may be?"

"Let's just say our relationship wasn't the best."

"Did he hit you?" Collins took the blanket lying behind him and handed it to her.

"What?" she asked, puzzled. "No, he never touched me."

"Where did those dents in the wall come from, Ms. Myers?"

"Those were here when we moved in, along with everything else wrong with this place."

"Now you said Robert tried staying at work as long as possible?" Collins flipped back a page on his pad. "What did he do?"

"He was a realtor." She looked at the apartment. "Not a very good one—look where we ended up."

Jones broke in with a wild expression on his face. "Robert Armes, I knew that name sounded familiar. I couldn't place it." He looked from Collins to Lindsey.

"Care to elaborate?" Collins sounded agitated from losing his momentum with the interrogation.

"Sorry, sir, but Robert Armes, if that's the same person I think it is. He sold me my house."

"How is that relevant?" Collins sounding more annoyed than ever.

"That was two days ago."

"The only thing that points out is your negligence. If this is the same Robert Armes, and it sounds like it is, you had the man involved in all this right in front of your ignorant face and didn't know it. Bravo." He clapped sarcastically as Jones shrunk ten feet.

"I'm sorry," Collins turned back to Lindsey. "We could have stopped this a long time ago if it wasn't for the carelessness of this young detective." He eyed Jones, who stood in the corner as if in a timeout.

"Now, your husband." Collins tried to regain some momentum he lost.

"Ex-husband," Lindsey corrected him.

"Right, did he come home with any damages to a vehicle?"

"No, well, yes, but from a deer almost a week ago. He used a rental while our car was being fixed."

"Oh, what kind might that be?"

"A Honda Pilot, but he returned it and brought back a 2008 Envoy." She rubbed her head, trying to remember the correct make and model.

"Did he happen to get it on Thursday?" Collins questioned.

"As a matter of fact, he did. He told me it was due to some electrical problem.

"I don't suppose you saw the SUV for confirmation?" Collins folded his notepad and placed it back in his jacket.

"I did, but I couldn't tell you the difference between an Envoy and a Pilot." She buried her head in her chest. "I should have known, he was acting so strangely. I thought he was cheating on me, I had no idea anything like this was happening."

Collins rested his hand on her shoulder. "It's OK." He tried to sound sympathetic. "Thank you for your time."

"Will you let me know something, if you find him?" She looked up at Collins with a worried expression. "I don't feel safe right now."

"These men will stay with you until we catch your husband, ma'am."

"Ex," Lindsey looked away. "Thank you."

"Come on, Jones"

"Where are we going?" he asked, ready to redeem himself.

"We are going to catch this son of a gun."

He walked back out the door where the crowd was growing.

"How are we going to manage that? This man could be going anywhere. Do you want me to put out a bolo on him?"

"Sure, if it'll make you feel better." Collins opened his car door.

Jones stopped. "You know where he's going, don't you?"

"Not yet." Collins started the car up as Jones sunk into the passenger seat. "But I will in a couple of minutes." Collins pulled out of the street and back toward the dealership.

This time, he was going to get everything he needed.

Chapter 13

Robert drove on edge, glancing in his rearview mirror every three seconds to be sure he wasn't followed. He didn't dare travel the interstate, fearful of being recognized by a cop.

Where am I going? he thought, heartbeat pounding.

He knew just the spot, where nobody would find him. He took a hard right, almost missing the turn off down the country road he traveled far too many times to count.

"What do you mean, you know where he's going?" Jones asked for the umpteenth time as Collins pulled back into the dealership.

Collins didn't bother to answer. He marched through the door, not stopping for the salesman coming his way. He walked behind the counter, pass the EMPLOYEES ONLY sign and busted open a door that read, MANAGER.

How dare you!" Earl jumped from behind his desk.

"I need something."

"I gave you everything you asked for earlier." Earl sunk back down into his seat, trying to gain some ounce of authority from the detective standing across from him.

"I'm asking for something different this time."

"What?"

"Do you keep tabs on your cars?"

"What?"

"Do you have GPS locater on all your rented vehicles?" Collins asked again, growing impatient.

"Not all of them."

"Which ones do you have them for?" Collins walked around the desk.

"Any model above 2005."

"Good, I need you to activate one."

"That's against regulations unless the car was stolen."

"Screw regulations."

"I'm sorry, but I can't and won't do it. I could get sued for everything I own." Earl stood, only coming to Collins shoulder as he did.

"This car was stolen, idiot," Collins lied.

"I didn't get a report." The manger stood his ground best he could.

"I'm here to give you that report."

"I need an official document stating the car was indeed stolen."

"Look." Collins stood taller than ever. "This man not only stole a car but was involved in a homicide. Now if you want to help a killer find his way to freedom, wait for your warrant."

"I'm sorry, I can't."

Collins reached for his hand cuffs. "You're under arrest."

"For what!" Earl shrieked.

"For obstructing an investigation."

"How dare you!"

"The same car which didn't get logged was involved in a hit and run. Since you didn't record the information, and lied about it, that's a crime right there. Now you have two choices. You can either help me by pressing a few buttons on your computer. Or help yourself into a nice pair of handcuffs." Collins dangled the metal bracelets in front of him.

"What's the license plate number?"

"You have it on file."

"It's quicker if I know the numbers, rather than sifting through the database." Earl woke his computer up.

"I don't have it, but I do have the name of the person who rented the car."

"Let's have it." Earl pulled up the mainframe to the company's database.

"Robert Armes."

Earl pecked away at the computer and waited a few minutes while the information loaded. "A 2008 Envoy?" Earl waited for approval.

"That's it. Where is he?"

"It takes a few minutes to locate." Earl leaned back in his chair.

"How long?" Collins asked pacing the office.

"Five minutes, if you're lucky."

"You had better hope this is your lucky day," Collins barked.

Robert pulled back into the driveway quickly, gravel dancing around his car as he inched closer toward the house. He drove through the grass and parked behind the residence, away from view of the road.

He jumped out of the car and grabbed his suitcase, tossing it on the ground next to the back door. He then picked up some blue tarp lying in the backyard and draped it across the Envoy, covering it completely. He raced back to the house, picked up his bags, and ran inside, making his way quickly up to the bedroom he had spent so many days trying to fix. He grabbed the hammer next to the wall and a handful of nails and rushed back downstairs.

Robert took a breather before he nailed shut the front entrance. Nobody could get through.

The only way in and out of the house was through the back door. A broken kitchen fridge barricaded anyone from entering there.

This was his only place of refuge now.

"Got it!" Earl said as his computer screen beeped.

"Where is he?" Collins was chomping at the bit, ready to find the person he'd been chasing for the past four days.

Earl punched a couple of keys on his keyboard and an address popped up. "He's down Whittin Lane. The car isn't moving." He studied the screen. "Mr. Armes is parked off on the side of the road somewhere."

"Can you get a better fix?" Collins hunched over the chair to look at the monitor.

"Hold on." Earl tapped again at the keyboard. "One-two-five Whittin Lane—he's at somebody's house."

Why does that place sound so familiar? Collins wondered. He shook off the old memory. "Jones," he yelled as he walked out of Earl's office. "I need you to get every bit of information you can about one-two-five Whittin Lane, and I want it now."

"I need a computer."

"Here." Collins turned the monitor of the desktop sitting on the counter. "Use this."

Jones went around the small door, which separated employees from customers and began typing away. "One twenty-five Whittin Lane," Jones said to himself as he keyed the address. The computer loaded the information.

"There was a man who lived there many years ago but has passed away. It was repossessed by the bank and then bought out by a local realtor company. They went out of business about a month and a half ago. Now it belongs to Robert Armes. Why would he be living in an apartment in Streamer Avenue if he owns this place?" Jones looked at the computer screen again to make sure he read the information correctly. "He should have known we could trace this back to him."

Collins rubbed his chin, the old memory popped into his head again. He remembered why the address sounded familiar. "People do stupid things when there're scared. They don't think straight." He pushed away his thoughts once more. "Come on, let's go."

Collins walked to the car. This time Jones got there first. He wasn't in any hurry to get back to this place.

"Take this right," Jones said as they pulled down the country road.

"I know where it is." Collins looked at the speedometer. He was going ten miles below the limit.

"It's just you're driving slower than usual, that's all."

"I know where to go," Collins repeated as he drew closer to the countryside home.

They rode the rest of the way in silence until pulling in the driveway. "I want you to take the front, I'm going to go around back," Collins ordered as he parked twenty feet from the house.

"Yes, sir." Jones voice shook a little.

"Have you done this before, son?" Collins looked over at his shaking hand.

"I've never shot at anyone before."

"Maybe you won't have to today." Collins grabbed for his gun. "Just stay steady, and don't panic."

They slid out of the car, keeping low to the ground. Jones slowly made his way to the front as Collins circled around back.

Robert stood at the window in the upstairs room looking down at the car that pulled up. He watched as the two men got out. *How did they find me?* His heart began beating faster than ever before. *What am I going to do?* He searched frantically for anything to use as a weapon.

The only thing useful was the hammer. He picked it up and watched as one of the men went around back, the other to the front. No way out. Robert stepped back from view of the window. A thought came to him.

Collins went to the back door, memories were starting to flash through his mind but he pushed them away. He noticed the blue tarp resting on something with wheels. Collins knew what it was without looking underneath.

"Robert!" he yelled. "Robert, we've got you surrounded, come out with your hands up." Collins knew he wouldn't—the guilty never did.

Collins stood beside the backdoor, ready to open and charge in. Then he heard a crash from the side of the house. "Jones!" Worry raced over his body for his partner. "Jones, are you OK?"

There was no answer.

"Jones, answer me!" But still nothing. Collins walked slowly toward the side of the building to the sound of the crash.

"I'm OK," he heard Jones finally yell from the opposite side of the house.

"What was that?" Just as he spoke, it happened again. Collins jumped back as small pieces of sheetrock were falling from the second story window. Collins leaned against the side of the building to keep from getting hit.

"Are you OK?" Collins heard Jones holler as he came around the side to check the source of the noise.

"I'm fine, stay back!" Collins looked up at the window. There was no one there.

"Get back to the front of the house," he yelled as he rushed the opposite way. They needed to keep the only two exits secured.

Robert raced from the window as he dropped the second piece of sheetrock to the ground, missing intentionally. He couldn't afford another murder on his hands, at least not one on purpose. Robert took the stairs two at a time and came dashing through the front of the house to the wooden door. He didn't care about how he nailed the entrance shut, he ran at it full blast. The door gave way. He had to reach the detective's car and get away. He stumbled onto the porch just as Jones came running from the side of the building.

"Freeze!" he yelled, stopping to take aim.

Robert kept going, there was no way he was going to stop. He ran down the steps tripping on the second one, the broken one. He face planted into the gravel.

"I said freeze," he heard as Jones came closer. Collins appeared from behind the building.

Robert lay there. *This is it*, he thought, as the cops got closer.

"You are under arrest for the murder of Jaime Mason." Collins came down on Robert, making sure he couldn't move. "Cuff him, Jones."

Jones pulled out a pair of handcuffs and came to the rescue.

"I didn't do it," Robert protested. He didn't struggle to get free anymore.

"You have the right to remain silent, anything you say, can and will be used against you in the court of law. You have a right to an attorney..." The detective's voiced trailed off as Robert was being pulled away.

It's over, Robert kept on thinking, *everything is over*.

Chapter 14

Robert was being led into an interrogation room. The place was dark, held up by three blank walls except the one-way mirror opposite him. A table with a manila envelope and two chairs rested opposite each other in the middle of the floor.

"Sit down." Collins pushed Robert into his seat.

Robert sat on edge.

"You are going to tell me everything I want to know."

Jones stood silently in the corner.

Good cop, bad cop, Robert thought, as stories and alibis swarmed his head. *They don't have anything on me, I was careful. I don't care what they say.*

"Where were you last Thursday morning around two thirty?"

"Why don't you tell me?"

"I'll tell you where." The detective reached for the envelope on the table. He pulled out a black and white picture of an SUV at a stoplight. "You were two blocks away from your hit and run." Collins nosed flared in anger.

"Well, seems like you've got it all figured out." Robert tried sounding nonchalant, "what do you need me for?"

"I need a confession, for the record." Collins looked up at the video camera recording every move.

"I'm sorry, but I don't know what you are talking about."

"Why did you run?"

"When I see a cop, I run, it's a reflex." Robert tried defending himself, sweating bullets now.

"Why would anyone run if they weren't guilty of something punishable by law?" Collins sat down in the empty chair. "So tell me, what are you guilty of?"

"Not murder."

"OK, then what?"

"I'm innocent."

"Then why did you run."

"Reflex."

"Your wife, well ex-wife by now, gave you up."

"She's lying."

"Why would she do something like that?" Collins leaned in closer.

"Because I was out, cheating on her that night." Robert didn't look away from the detective.

"Uh huh. With who?"

"You met her today at the funeral, Rebecca Downing, the redhead. Why would I go to the funeral of the woman I supposedly murdered?" Robert tried the sympathy card. "Why would I sit there, hand in hand with the daughter of the woman who was buried just four hours ago? What kind of person do you think I am?"

"The kind of person who kills and tries to get away with it." Collins leaned over the table, inches away from Robert's face. "That's not going to happen."

"You don't have any proof!" Robert waited anxiously for an answer.

"On the contrary, we have plenty of proof." Collins fell back in his chair.

"Let me see it," Robert demanded. *What could they have?* he thought, *I was extremely careful.*

"Well, after we match your voice with the recording from the nine-one-one call using this little chat we're having for comparison, we can place you at the scene of the crime. Oh, and we also have the tire tracks, which match the exact same make and brand on your vehicle—not to mention your wife's confession, and a couple more things we're just waiting on the lab to prove."

Robert went into frantic mode. "OK, OK, I admit I was there on the same night, but I didn't hit this woman. I found her there. Yes, I called nine-one-one, but that's not what happened."

"What happened?"

"I had been drinking. I had been cheating on my wife. I wasn't thinking clearly. I was on my way home when I went by the school. I saw something on the ground. I thought it was a deer. Then it started moving. That's when I slammed on the brakes. I got out of the car and went to the payphone and dialed nine-one-one."

"Why didn't you wait? Why didn't you explain yourself to the police who showed up?"

"There were no witnesses. It was just me, with alcohol on my breath. What do you think would have happened?" Robert's left eye twitched.

"That's a good story." Collins got up to leave. "Well-rehearsed."

"It's true!" Robert shouted in anger and fear.

"Well, let's see what Rebecca has to say." Collins walked out the door. Jones followed.

"You know, he has a point." Jones kept in step with Collins as he walked down the hallway. "Without any witnesses, it's all circumstantial."

"I know." Collins took the flight of stairs up to the main floor. "I know."

"What are we going to do?"

"Get the truth." Collins reached in his pocket and pulled out his cell phone. He shuffled through the list of recent calls until he found the one he was looking for.

"Hello?" Rebecca answered with a softness in her voice from hours of crying.

"Ms. Rebecca Downing?"

"Yes, yes, this is Rebecca. Who is this?"

"Detective Collins."

There was a quick pause on the other line and the sound of movement, as if she stood up. "Did you find him?"

"We do have a suspect, but we need your help with some time issues."

"Of course, but I don't see how I can help?" There was more noise on the other end. Another woman's voice was heard in the background.

"Why don't you come down to the station and we'll talk about this face to face." Collins spoke softly but sternly.

"I'll be there in ten minutes," Rebecca said. There was a soft click as she hung up.

"You want to fill me in?" Jones asked curiously.

"You'll find out in about ten minutes," Collins said as he opened the bottom drawer of his desk to reach for something.

"What is it you need from me?" Rebecca asked as she came rushing through the station's doors. A woman followed on her heels.

"Why don't you take a minute to calm yourself before I take you downstairs?" Collins put a steady hand on her shoulder.

"I don't need to rest. I need answers."

"Who is this lady with you? A sister?" He eyed the woman behind her.

"What? No. I'm an only child. This is the lady from the funeral. She's the one who interrupted our conversation." Rebecca turned to give a weak smile at the woman to show she wasn't offended.

"I don't recall." Collins thought back to the funeral and then to Robert. "I'm Detective Phil Collins," he introduced himself, stalling for time while Rebecca caught her breath.

"Tiffany Mouser," the brunette responded as she shook his hand.

"How did you know the deceased?"

"It's a long story."

"Come on, I want to see the man who murdered my mother." Rebecca took off, not knowing where she was going.

Collins took her down the staircase and down the hall, right outside the room where Robert was sitting. He stopped and turn toward Rebecca. "There is something you should know before you see this man."

"What?" Rebecca looked alarmed.

"The suspect we have was also at the funeral."

"What? Who? That son of a—" but she was cut off.

"It's the same man you were with." Collins waited for her expression.

"What are you talking about? I wasn't with anyone." Rebecca was thinking hard. "Well, Robert was there."

Collins didn't say anything but waited.

"Robert?" her eyes lit up and jaw dropped. "No, there must be some mistake—he wouldn't, he couldn't. Why would he?"

"We are trying to figure that out, but I need to ask you something before we go in."

"What?" Rebecca leaned against the wall for support.

"Was Robert with you the night of the incident?"

"Yes."

"About what time?"

190

"I don't know. It was late." Rebecca sank further into the wall.

"Can you give me an estimate?"

"I'm sorry, I don't know, but it couldn't have been Robert." She sounded less sure this time. "It couldn't."

Jones stood silently. Tiffany reached out to grab Rebecca's wrist for comfort. "You don't have to go in, you know." Tiffany looked into her eyes.

"She's right." Jones piped in.

"No, I want to do this. I need to see this with my own eyes." She looked up at Collins. "Do you have any proof?"

"Yes."

"May I see it?" She asked, trying to stand taller against the wall.

"No, not yet."

"Why couldn't you tell me this over the phone? Why did you need me to come down here?"

"I thought you might want to see the man who murdered your mother." Collins looked at her with soft eyes.

"That's not the only reason why, is it?" Tiffany spoke, looking from Jones to Collins.

"No," Collins admitted. "I think maybe you could get a confession from him."

"Why do you need a confession if you have proof?" Rebecca's face was white.

"The evidence we have isn't as concrete as we would like. If we go to court, it may not be enough to convict him."

191

"I don't know what I can do."

"You can try," Jones spoke up again.

"I might lose it in there." She backed up off the wall. "If this man did what you said he did, I don't know if I can keep it together."

"I'll help you." Tiffany looked from Jones to Collins as if waiting for any objections then she turned back to Rebecca. "It feels like I lost a mother too."

"I'll try," was all Rebecca said.

"OK." Collins stood back. "We will be right on the other side of the window if you need anything."

Rebecca and Tiffany hugged each other for support before they went in to face their fear.

Robert looked up as the doorknob turned slowly, his eyes wide, his heart pumped faster. "What are you doing here?" he asked, trying to sound calm. Rebecca didn't look at him. She walked over to the mirror, holding Tiffany's hand for support.

"Is it true?" Rebecca spoke to the window rather than facing Robert.

"Is what true?"

"Don't play games with me!" Rebecca's voice sounded more hostile with every word she spoke. "Why are you here?"

"I don't know."

"Did you know her?" Rebecca spoke again to the window.

"What are you talking about?" Robert looked up at the back of Rebecca's head.

"What happened?"

"I'm sorry, I don't know what you are talking about."

"How could you come to her funeral?" Rebecca turned toward the man in the chair. "How could you do this to her, to me?" Her voice was getting louder, starting to shriek.

"Rebecca, what are you talking about?" Robert tried keeping calm. His insides were screaming at him to tell the truth. His body ached with the pain of keeping all the lies inside.

"Why did you do this to me?" She let go of Tiffany's hand and leaned on the table.

"What are you talking about? I told you I don't know why I'm here. It's all just a big misunder—"

"How dare you!" Rebecca slapped Robert across the face, leaving a red handprint on his cheek.

There was a soft tap at the window.

"What did you do that for?" Robert tried sounding hurt and surprised. "I told you, I don't know what you are talking about."

Rebecca lost control. "How dare you!" she screamed as she jumped across the table, knocking Robert and the chair over. "How dare you!" She slapped as hard as she could at his face.

Robert hollered in pain and shock but didn't move. *I deserve this*, he thought. *All the pain I've caused everybody.*

Tiffany tried to pull Rebecca off as she swung harder with her fist. The side door burst open and Collins and Jones rushed to pull the hysterical woman off the bloodied man on the floor.

"It was an accident," Robert mumbled as he drifted slowly out of consciousness.

"Joshua!" Lindsey yelled from the porch. "Joshua Tyler Armes."

Joshua stopped kicking a soccer ball in the yard and turned to face his mother.

"What did I tell you about sharing with your little sister?" She held the hand of a small five-year-old by her side.

"I was."

Joshua lied like little kids do.

"If you were, then why do you still have the ball? I don't want to have to tell you again. Go ahead, sweetie," she leaned down to the big-eyed five-year-old, eyes like her father, and said, "go play with your big brother."

The little girl walked down the three steps by herself, using the railing for support.

Lindsey went back to sit on the swing dangling from the porch roof. "You could have chimed in any time you know," she positioned herself next to Robert, who was grinning from ear to ear.

"Looked like you had everything under control." He kissed her head as she leaned back into him.

"Your son is just like you, stubborn and headstrong."

"Well, Armes men are. I thought you found that attractive about me?"

"No, it was your kind heart and gentle smile." She stared out at the kids; Joshua had let Julie kick the ball. "It was the stubbornness which almost made me leave you at the altar."

"Well, lucky for me you changed your mind." Robert rested his head on hers.

"Yeah, lucky me," she smiled. "Now you're going to take Joshua to the game this evening while I prepare supper, right? Mom is coming over tonight to teach me how to make her pot roast, the stuff you like so much." She patted his stomach.

"All right, can't wait," Robert exclaimed.

"Make sure you tape the whole game, too. I want to watch it when you all get back."

"I'll catch every moment. I could be the next Steven Spielberg."

"You wish," Lindsey chuckled. "I'm serious though, don't miss a step."

"I know, honey," Robert reassured her. "I can't believe he is already eight years old."

"I know," Lindsey sighed. "They are growing up so fast."

"Well, isn't that why we had them. So they could take care of us?" Robert propped his feet up in the swing as Lindsey readjusted herself.

"Yeah, would be nice." She fell further into his arms.

What a perfect Sunday afternoon, Robert thought as the kids laughed in the yard.

Chapter 15

"When do you think he'll be awake?" A familiar voice echoed off the walls as Robert started coming back into consciousness.

"I don't know. He was hit pretty hard," a man answered. "We'll have to wait and see."

"I just want to get this over with," the woman's voice grew closer.

Robert opened his eyes to a man with a stethoscope dangling around his neck. "Where am I?" He tried to speak, but his voice was sore.

"You are at the medical station." The doctor checked his vitals as Robert tried to move, but something pulled him back. He looked over, his eyes focused on a metal pair of handcuffs hanging on the side of the rail.

"How long will it be before we can do this?" The familiar woman's voice belonged to Lindsey.

"About ten minutes." The doctor wrapped his fingers around Robert's free wrist to check his heart rate.

"I'll wait outside." Lindsey turned to leave.

"What's going on?" Robert's head was throbbing.

"Sit still." The doctor pushed him back on the bed.

"Where am I?"

"The police station, now cough." The physician placed the stethoscope on his chest.

Robert mustered a weak cough.

"All right, that should do it." The doctor handed some pills in a plastic cup to Robert. "For the headache."

Robert took it slowly and swallowed without water.

The doctor turned to leave "He's all yours," Robert heard him say outside the door. He was replaced by Lindsey, who looked tired and emotionally exhausted.

"Don't speak." Lindsey held up a hand to stop him. "I came to let you know I'm leaving." Lindsey didn't look directly at Robert but above his head at the wall. "I've packed all my things and I'm leaving. You can have everything, the apartment, the furniture, everything. You should expect to hear from a divorce attorney soon."

"Where are you going?"

"It doesn't matter."

"Why did you come here? You could have told me this over the phone."

"I needed to find out something."

"What do you want to know" Robert asked, already defeated.

Lindsey stalled for a moment and then spoke. "I want to know why you cheated on me."

Robert looked at her stunned. He wasn't expecting this.

"We weren't happy," he responded through swollen lips.

"Yeah, we weren't, but I was willing to work at our marriage, though. Through all the good and bad, I was still willing to try. I thought I showed you that."

There was nothing else to do but agree. "You did."

"Then why?"

"I'm sorry."

"Me too." Lindsey turned to leave.

"It was an accident," Robert called out.

"Don't tell me that." She stood in the doorway. "Goodbye, Robert." She walked out the door and out of his life.

Collins sat at his desk and pulled a small brown envelope, no bigger than an index card, from his pocket. He wanted to look at this earlier, before Rebecca had gotten here, but didn't have time. It had been sitting at the bottom of his desk drawer for years now, only taken out in times of great sorrow or misery, to remind him of where he came from. He flipped through the pictures staring at each one with intensity and care, all in black and white and all of his childhood.

They were of his parents, smiling on a wooden porch they had built with their bare hands. Another of him and his brother playing football in the front yard, and one of them chasing their dog Shadow around, laughing the whole time.

Collins turned over the last photo. This was the one he was looking for. He fingered the edges of the old border, careful not to bend or tear the fragile memory.

There were two kids in the photograph—two boys, no older than ten, sitting on the steps taking their annual picture like they did every summer. He had forgotten who had taken the picture, probably his mom or dad, but he didn't forget the reason why he was smiling.

Collins pressed his index finger on the face of a younger him, his arms draped across the nape of his younger brother. This was the first picture they had taken in front of the house their father had built, piece by piece. His family had moved out of a small rundown apartment building into a countryside home.

"Sir." Jones was waving to get his attention.

"What is it?" Collins rose from his chair, sticking the old photos carefully into the envelope and back into his bottom drawer.

"Armes is awake, sir."

"Well, it's about time. Where are those two women?"

"There waiting outside the medical station now." Jones moved toward the stairwell.

"Good." Collins took the stairs at a fast pace, considering his age. "We're going to end this now."

He walked down the hallway toward the medical wing. "Ms. Downing, Ms. Mouser, I want you to stay here for a minute while I speak with Mr. Armes alone. That means you too." He looked over his shoulder at Jones.

"I'll be at the door." Jones stood at the entrance as his boss walked in.

Collins spotted Robert lying handcuffed to a bed at the end of the row.

The police station had a decent medical wing, considering their size. It was fully equipped with the necessities in case of an emergency and always had a trained physician around. Even though there were only four beds, they were rarely ever used.

"I want the truth," Collins spoke as he stood beside Robert.

"I told you I didn't do anything," Robert said with a hoarse whisper.

"Then why did you tell me it was an accident before you passed out?" Collins leaned in to hear every word.

"I was talking about my marriage."

"Oh, come on," Collins raised his voice. "You and I both know that's not true. We have the proof right upstairs."

"Then you'll have no problem convicting me in court."

"I want to tell you a story," Collins spoke softly, as if recalling the information of the tale.

Robert didn't say anything.

"When I was a little boy, my parents didn't have a lot of money. My father worked two jobs to feed my mother, brother, and myself. Mom stayed home and made sure we had an education. Times were tough."

"My father was a great man, stern, strong, and self-motivated. He worked five years to save up enough money to buy a spot of land on the outskirts of town. Enough room to grow a small garden for food, and enough room for me and my brother to run."

"A year went by. My father would get up early on his days off and go to that spot of land and start work on building a house for his family. Every free second he was out there until it was done. Those seven years prior our new home was the hardest for our family. We had to ration everything. Nothing got thrown away. Other kids would laugh at us and call us poor, trashy, everything under the sun. The only way we got through it was by sticking together."

Robert stared at the ceiling.

"When I was around ten years old, we moved to our new place, our new life. Everything was great, smiles all day. We had room to grow; my brother and I were now able to have separate rooms. Regardless, we shared one, that's how close we were. Every day was a fresh start."

Collins turned his back toward Robert and spoke to the empty room.

"I visited that house today for the first time in nearly thirty-five years. I promised myself I would never go back, but I did today."

Robert continued to stare up at the lights in the paneled ceiling.

"One day something happened. My younger brother was in the army, so he was away at the time. I had just started working here at the station. My mother and father were out eating like they did every Wednesday night, right here in town. They were walking back to their vehicle. A kid, no older than yourself, had gotten behind the wheel of a car."

Robert knew where this was going.

"He ran right into my mom and dad and killed them both instantly." Collins clenched his fist together. "I chased that man down, but there wasn't enough evidence to put him away. Just like your story, there weren't any witnesses around. I knew he had done it and gotten away. I never healed completely. That anger controlled me for the longest time. Later, I received news my brother had died in battle, not even a week later. Just like that, I was alone. I had lost everybody in my family in one week, everyone I had ever loved, and everyone who loved me."

Robert felt a tear in the corner of his eye, but he didn't dare look at Collins.

"Do the right thing and don't destroy someone's life because you're afraid of what might happen, because you are afraid to tell the truth."

Robert didn't move.

Collins didn't say another word. He walked back toward the exit and out the room.

"What did he say?" Rebecca jumped up as soon as Collins walked through the door.

"Nothing useful," he spat out.

"I want to talk to him." Rebecca stood tall.

"I don't think that's a good idea," Jones cut in, "considering last time."

"I'll control myself." Rebecca tried to look confident, but her tone gave it away.

"I don't think so." Collins ended it.

"Fine, why don't you or Jones come in and babysit me?"

"No," Collins barked.

"I'll do it," Jones spoke from the doorway. "I'll make sure neither one of them gets hurt."

Collins said nothing.

Rebecca took the silence as an opportunity to grab Jones' wrist and pull him in behind her, leaving Tiffany and Collins alone outside in the waiting room.

Robert heard the door open again. He tensed up, thinking Collins had returned with a bat. *Maybe I should be honest*, Robert thought, as two sets of footsteps clamored against the concrete floor.

"I want the truth."

He turned to see Rebecca marching across the room, Jones right beside her.

"I told the truth," Robert blurted out, covering his broken face with his free hand.

"That's far enough." Jones grabbed at Rebecca's hand. "You aren't getting any closer. You want to talk, talk."

"Bull crap." Rebecca stood out of striking distant. "I want to know what really happened that night."

"I was with you."

Rebecca flinched as the thought crossed her mind.

"Tell me the truth," she demanded.

Robert's mind was racing. "I want a deal."

"What?"

"I want a deal, in writing. I will tell you everything I know for no court time opened to the public. No spectacle made, no one outside this room will know who I am and no jail time."

"Can you do that?" Rebecca turned toward Jones.

"I'd have to talk with Collins, who would then have to talk to the captain, who'd talk with the judge and the prosecutor," Jones answered.

"Make that happen," Robert spoke loudly to get his point across. "I will tell you everything you want to know, everything."

Rebecca raced out of the room.

"What are you doing?" Jones chased after her.

"Getting that deal."

"You want to do what?" Collins shouted as Rebecca ran out to the medical station relaying the information.

"I want to know the truth. I want to cut a deal with him."

"I'm sorry, but there is no way we are cutting a deal with this man." He turned to walk away.

"This case involves me. She was my mother and this is what I want to do."

"This man is a murderer." Collins whipped around.

"Yes, I know, but I also know you don't have enough evidence to convict him." She stared at him with a determined stance and piercing eyes.

"I need more time."

"You can only hold him for so long. I want to know the truth before he walks. I need to know the truth."

"You can't be sure what he says is the truth."

"Maybe not, but it's all I have." Her eyes started to tear up. "I need to know, for my mother, I need to know."

"I don't like it." Collins met her tearful gaze.

"How long will it take for a deal to come through?" She glanced over her shoulder toward the medical room.

"I'll see what I can do." Collins turned to leave but stopped to look back at Rebecca. "Are you sure this is what you want to do?"

"More than anything," she answered.

Collins returned an hour later with a sheet of paper in his hand.

"You got the deal?" Rebecca stood.

"No."

"What?" Rebecca looked at his hands. "What's that?"

"This is a document for his arraignment tomorrow." Collins held it out for her to see.

She pushed the paper away. "What about the deal?"

"The D.A. didn't go for it."

"Sir?" Jones spoke from where he was sitting. "You know we have nothing on him."

Collins glared in his direction. "That's for the court to decide."

"So what?" Rebecca looked from Jones to Collins, "if he isn't convicted, he'll walk."

"Yeah," Jones answered her.

Rebecca stormed back into the medical wing. Jones, Tiffany, and Collins right behind her.

"I want to know the truth!" she yelled at Robert, who lifted himself up as far as the handcuffs would allow.

"The deal didn't go through?" He already knew the answer by the tone of her voice.

"Tell me everything I want to know and I'll make sure it's known in court," she pleaded with him.

Robert hesitated. *How much do they really have on me*, he wondered as everyone stared at him. "I already told you the truth."

"Why did you want the deal if nothing happened?" Rebecca stomped her foot in anger.

"Because none of you believe me. This was my only shot of getting out of here, even though I'm innocent. Whatever you have on me are lies. I didn't do anything!"

Rebecca moved to pounce on him again but Jones held her back. "Liar!" she screamed as she pulled to get free.

"Get her out of here," Collins yelled at Jones.

Jones, with help from Tiffany, forced her back out into the waiting room.

"Your arraignment is at nine tomorrow morning." He handed the document for Robert to take. "Don't be late."

A chubby officer escorted Robert to the county jail to remain in custody until his arraignment.

He sat on the bed in the small holding area and leaned his head against the cement wall, using one of the pillows given to him for support.

He knew he was going to prison. There was no way out of it.

The lights switched off as the station shut down for the night. There were two guards outside the holding room. Each alternated shifts while watching over their guests for the night.

Robert stared out, not focusing or thinking of anything in particular. He closed his eyes to escape for a few minutes. Hours passed as he breathed in and out, falling into a deep sleep.

"Everything's all packed." Robert slammed the trunk of the car. "I checked the oil and the air in the tires. You're good to go, honey."

"Thanks, Dad," Julie said as she hugged her father.

"Now, I want you to call when you get there," Lindsey spoke through soft tears.

"Mom," Julie protested, "I'm twenty-two years old. I think I'm old enough to make it somewhere without having to call my mommy when I reach my destination." She went and hugged her anyways.

"I don't care how old you get, you'll always be my little girl." Lindsey squeezed her daughter tight.

"How long of a drive is it?" Robert asked the question he already knew the answer to.

"It's about five hours." Julie let go of her mom and went to hug her dad.

"Are you sure you couldn't find a job around here—you know you can stay as long as you want, rent free." He smiled down at his little girl.

"Dad," she groaned, "there's nothing here for me to do, nothing in my field. I thought that's why I went to college, to get away from this dying town."

"I thought you went to get away from me," he laughed softly.

"That was just a bonus," she smiled up at him.

"Here's some gas money." Robert reached for his wallet and pulled out five hundred dollars.

"Dad." Julie looked at the money, then back at her father. "Dad, this is more than enough for gas."

"Just take it. It's a little something to help you get started. It's not much."

"Thanks, Daddy." She hugged him again. "I love you."

"I love you too." He was about to cry. "Come here, Lindsey." He pulled her over. She had a tearstained napkin in her hand. "Group hug."

They stood there for about five minutes, holding on tightly to one another.

"OK, I have to get going," Julie broke off.

"You sure you can't stay for one more day?" Lindsey protested.

"I start work tomorrow morning, and I still have a lot of unpacking to do."

"Be safe, sweetie," she called as Julie hopped into her car.

"Make sure you get that oil changed every three thousand miles," Robert called after her as the engine roared.

"I love you, honey," Lindsey spoke through more tears.

The car started to move away. A small hand was sticking out the side, waving goodbye.

"I can't believe our little girl is gone." Lindsey leaned into Robert.

"I know." Robert rested his head on hers, comforting her and himself at the same time.

"That was our last child, flying from the nest."

"I know." Robert rubbed her shoulder.

"What are we going to do with this big old house?" She turned and stared at the two-story country home.

"Whatever you want to do." He smiled at her as they walked hand and hand back up the stairs and onto the porch.

"I love you, honey," Robert spoke softly into her ear.

She reached up and kissed him.

They walked over and sat on the porch swing, staring out at the stirred up gravel that was starting to settle back down.

Chapter 16

"Get up, it's time to go." The chubby guard clamored on the metal bars, waking his guest. "Here, put these on." He tossed an orange jumpsuit with *Department of Corrections* on the back at him.

Robert slowly got up, not ready for this day to come.

"I'll be back in ten minutes, you'd better be ready. The judge doesn't like being kept waiting." He walked back through the doors toward his office.

Robert slowly dressed, said a half-hearted prayer, and waited for the policeman to return.

"All right, you ready?" the keeper of keys asked as he unlocked the door.

Robert didn't say anything. He waited to be handcuffed.

"I'd imagine you'd get the death penalty for this one." The guard carried on a one way conversation with him. "Yeah, I don't see too many people get away with murder. In fact," he rubbed his chin, "I ain't never seen anyone get away with murder around here before."

Robert stared straight.

"Come on then." The guard pushed him forward from behind.

He walked down the hall past another holding cell identical to his own. The guard pushed him through two double doors. A man stood watch to make sure nobody came in or out. Robert marched into the morning sunshine and spotted his escort vehicle. Collins and Jones stood right beside it.

"We'll take it from here," Collins spoke as he reached out for Robert's wrist.

"Need you to sign for transportation." The chubby guard looked him over.

"Jones will take care of that for you." Collins pointed in his direction.

Jones followed the chubby man as he waddled back to the building, only to return a minute later.

"Are you ready?" Collins turned around in the driver's seat to look at Robert, a smug grin on his face.

Robert didn't say anything.

"Finally, justice." Collins started the car as Jones jumped in the passenger seat. "Now don't try anything funny," Collins spoke as he put the car in reverse.

What am I going to do, Robert thought, but he held his tongue. His hands were cuffed and his feet chained together.

"Here we go." Collins took off toward the courthouse.

Robert stared out the window, catching every glimpse of freedom passing by. There were kids playing on the sidewalk, too young to go to school. Their mothers watching attentively, making sure nothing happened to their little pride and joys. Robert watched the scenery with saddened eyes until his entourage slowed down and pulled in behind the courthouse.

Collins parked and hopped out. "Beautiful day," he said as he opened the door for Robert.

Robert didn't look him in the eye.

Collins walked him up the few stairs and through the back door. There was a routine body search in the walkway for all prisoners coming through. Robert didn't move as he was being patted down.

"All clear." The man who searched him gave the thumbs up sign to Collins, who grabbed him and pushed forward. "This way." Collins guided Robert toward another door reading KEEP CLOSED behind it, he was met with an empty courtroom.

"Sit here." Collins pushed him down onto an empty seat, taking the handcuffs off. "Your arraignment will begin in ten minutes." Collins took off and walked back the way he came, leaving Robert alone with security guards of the court.

Robert fidgeted a little as the time passed slowly. Suddenly, the doors opened at the end of the room and Rebecca walked in, followed by Tiffany, Collins, and Jones bringing up the rear.

Rebecca wore a dark blue skirt and jacket with a white blouse underneath. She looked professional and ready for this day to end. She walked down the aisle and took a seat on the left. Rebecca didn't look in Robert's direction.

Tiffany, Collins, and Jones filed into the seats beside her for moral support. Shortly after they entered, a couple of men and women with pens and pads came through the door.

The media is here, Robert thought as he turned, not wanting to face them. Everyone filed in and the courtroom entrance closed.

Here we go, Robert thought as his court-appointed attorney sat down beside him.

"All rise," the bailiff spoke loudly for the whole courtroom to hear. "The honorable Judge Thompson is residing."

Robert stood ready to plead "not guilty" when asked.

Judge Thompson appeared from a door behind the podium from whence he sat. He had gray hair and wrinkles that went on for miles. He wore the standard honorable black robe required for court. The judge sat in his chair, ready to begin the day with Robert.

"You may now be seated." The bailiff hollered.

"OK," Thompson began as if tired. "We are here on behalf of the deceased, Jaime Mason. Mr. Robert Cal Armes is the murder suspect of Jaime Marie Mason in involuntary vehicular manslaughter, Thursday morning at approximately 2:45 a.m. This caused severe internal damages that led to her death. Mr. Armes, how do you plead?" The judge looked over at Robert with weary eyes.

Robert stood. He could feel every pair of eyes focusing on him. Off in the corner, the sketch artist's hands flew up and down on a notepad, sketching him as fast as possible. His heart was pounding. *This is it*, he thought, *the moment has finally come*. He glanced at the judge, then sideways at Rebecca, whose eyes were focused so intently upon him, he could feel the burn of hatred emanating from her stare.

"Mr. Armes?" the Judge broke the silence of the courtroom. "Mr. Armes, how do you plead?"

Robert didn't move, thoughts of the accident were flashing so fast through his head, he thought he would pass out. He took a deep breath. "Your Honor," he was stalling for time. "I plead..." he closed his eyes, took a deep breath and said, "I plead guilty, Your Honor."

Robert could hear the gasps throughout the courtroom but he didn't dare open his eyes.

"Order, order," Judge Thompson bellowed, using his gavel to gain stability in the courtroom.

The room quieted down, but there were still bustles of noise from the pens being used and papers being turned by reporters.

"Bailiff," Thompson spoke with authority, "take this man into custody until sentencing for the murder of Jaime Marie Mason by involuntary vehicular manslaughter." He banged his gavel once again, this time for closure.

The man in the authoritative suit rushed over to Robert, handcuffed and pushed him off toward the same door he had entered.

Robert felt worse and better at the same time as he walked the hallway and back down the steps, into the morning sunshine.

"Mr. Armes, Mr. Armes," the reporters were waiting for him when he exited the building. Their microphones pressed into his face. "What happened, Mr. Armes? Can you give us some details about the murder?"

Robert drowned them out. All he could think of was how his life was over. No matter if he did the right thing by owning up to his mistakes, it cost him everything.

He was pushed into a different car and transported to the state prison, twenty miles away. Robert took every detail of the view outside. This was going to be the last thing he saw of the outside, of freedom, for a while.

The correctional officer at the prison took the metal bracelets off Robert as he showed him to his new home. "Enjoy your stay," he said sarcastically as he locked the door and turned to leave.

Robert walked to his bed and lay down on the hard mattress, the one he would be using for a good portion of his life. Robert closed his eyes, tried to escape everything that had happened. He had convicted himself without knowing what evidence was brought against him. Had given everything up to pay for the crime he accidentally committed, but he didn't feel much better.

Robert pounded the wall in anger. He never got a chance to tell Lindsey about the house, but he doubted she would care now anyways. *How could I have been so stupid?* His head was starting to hurt. *I never should have left that night.* He thought back to when he and Lindsey had fought over the fact he hit a deer. *I wonder if things would have turned out differently if I had just gone back into the apartment and never left.*

Robert tried to sleep, but the noise from the other inmates wouldn't allow him to. *I'll get used to it over time*, he thought as he tossed around on his bed, trying to get comfortable. *I'll get use to everything in time.* Robert gave up trying to relax and walked around the small cell for a couple hours while time slowly passed by.

He was already feeling claustrophobic when the guard who locked him up in this cage came back. "You have a visitor."

"What?"

"You have a visitor," the guard repeated, annoyed. "Turn with your back against the wall and hands above your head."

Robert did as told while the man handcuffed him. "Let's go." He pushed him out the door and guided him down the hall. Robert passed by cages identical to his, with other angry inmates in them. They continued walking, passing through a set of doors protected by another man in uniform.

The guard pushed him off to the right and through more doors into an empty room. "Sit here," he said and pushed him into the only chair in the small space. Then he walked back the way he came. Robert heard a click as the doorknob turned from the other side, locking him in.

Robert looked around the small room. It was poorly lit, and the walls were dingy gray, the same color as his cell. There was a desk in front of him and a glass window breaking the room in half. The other side was identical to his.

Who would come to visit me? Robert thought as he tapped on the desk in front of him nervously. His wife? Robert waited for what felt like hours until he saw the handle on the other side of the glass turn and the door sprung open slowly, hesitantly.

In walked Rebecca, her red hair hung loosely. She was wearing the same clothes from her court appearance, only not as neatly arranged as earlier. Following was her entourage, Collins, Tiffany, and Jones.

Robert took them in and then looked at Rebecca. Her eyes were weak, as if she hadn't slept in weeks, her mouth twitched a little at every move. She didn't look directly at Robert but off to the side, as if he wasn't there.

217

He waited for her to say something.

She sat waiting, thinking. Everybody else stood behind her, curious expressions on their faces.

Robert couldn't take it any longer. He didn't want to startle her but he had no choice. He wrapped his knuckles on the window.

She jumped a little and looked directly at him.

He could see there was a question in her eyes.

"What do you want to know?" Robert asked.

"I want to know everything. Every detail, every word, everything." She got up and paced the room with anticipation.

"I don't' know where to begin," Robert started. The memories had been flashing nonstop through his brain since the moment it happened.

"How 'bout from when you left my hotel?" She fidgeted a little.

Robert began his story.

"I was driving home, still buzzed from the drinks, and very upset about what happened with you. No offense," he looked up at her. "I lied to you too, except I'm married—was, divorced as of yesterday. You probably saw my wife and didn't recognize her."

"You son of a—you were married!" Rebecca screamed at him, losing it for the second time in two days. "You were married! You slimy, no good, rotten little—"

"I told you I was sorry, and I truly am," Robert cut into her name-calling. "Everything that happened that night was a mistake, a terrible horrible mistake I wish every second of everyday I could undo, but I can't."

Rebecca took in a deep painful breath. "Continue." She pursed her lips.

"Well, there was something going on at Jefferson Elementary School that night. Along with the alcohol, I wasn't thinking clearly, I wasn't concentrating, and then it happened. I thought I had hit a deer or something. I saw your mother move on the concrete, except I didn't know who she was, or even that she was a she. I panicked. There was nobody around. The police wouldn't have believed me with alcohol on my breath. I rushed to the payphone and dialed nine-one-one then went back to the car and drove off." He took a deep breath and continued. "I parked a couple blocks over and waited for help to show up before I left. I couldn't just leave her like I did."

"How could you go to her funeral? How could you go to the hospital with me?" Rebecca started crying.

"I didn't know your mother was the one I had hit when we went to the hospital." Robert too was getting teary eyed. "As far as the funeral, I thought if I came, I too could have closure. I too could be forgiven for what I had done."

"How dare you!" Tiffany butted in. "That woman deserved better."

"I know," Robert pleaded. I'm so sorry. I never meant for anything like this to happen."

"Jaime was the closest thing I had to a mother," Tiffany said. "I've had too much taken away from me already. She was all I had left." Rebecca came over to comfort her.

"Do you know what I've been through? I can't even celebrate my own birthday because my mother died while giving birth to me. My father," she was hysterical now, "My father died serving his country. He died before I was born. All I knew of him was his name—Jonathan Collins." Phil Collins' eyes lit up as Tiffany continued. "Jaime was already dying, but she didn't deserve to go like that. Nobody deserves to go like that." She broke down.

Did I hear right? Collins thought, as Tiffany finished her outburst. "Excuse me?" he interrupted. Tiffany, what did you say your father's name was?"

Tiffany looked up from Rebecca's shoulder. "What? Why?"

"Just what was his name?" Collins heart pounded harder.

"Jonathan Collins."

"Was he in the armed forces?"

"Yes, he served as a petty officer. Why?"

"Who was his wife?"

"What?"

"His wife. What was her name?"

"Rose Adams. What's going on?"

"When did your father die?"

"September 20."

"What year?"

"In 1980. What does this have to do with anything?" She stared at Collins.

"Do you know where your father was from?" Collins continued his own interrogation.

"He grew up around here, somewhere down Whittin Lane. What is going on?"

Collins heart was pumping so fast he couldn't hear anyone around him. *Could this be true?* he thought, the room was spinning.

"How did your father meet your mother?" Collins looked up at Tiffany, waiting for an answer.

"They met when he was on an army base in Texas. Now tell me what this is about, or I'm not answering anymore of your questions."

"My name is Phil Collins," was all he said.

"I know."

"I don't think you understand." Collins was at a loss for words. "My name is Phil Collins," he repeated, as if this was all that needed to be said.

"I think you need to lie down" Jones grabbed his wrist.

"No, no, don't you see," he jerked his hand away.

"What are you talking about?" Rebecca asked. "You have the same last names?"

"Yes."

"I'm not following." Tiffany's face was in a state of worry.

"I had a brother whose name was Jonathan Eric Collins," Phil said, astounded he wasn't getting his point across.

"Yeah, so?" Rebecca sounded just as confused as Tiffany.

"My brother served in the military. He trained on a base in Texas and he died September 20, 1980."

Rebecca and Tiffany gasped as Jones stumbled in shock.

"Does this mean what I think?" Tiffany asked.

"I think it does." Collins smiled for the first time since he could remember. All the worries of the case, all the bad memories of what happened to his parents and his brother had escaped him for a brief moment in time.

"Are you my uncle?" Tiffany stood still.

"I'm sure we could do a simple DNA test and see, but I think so." Collins held out his arms for a hug but Tiffany didn't move.

"Are you serious?" she asked dumbstruck.

"I can't believe it, either." Collins walked over and embraced her, something he hadn't done to anyone in years.

For the first time in a long time, Collins had someone to call family again.

"I need to know something." Rebecca turned back toward the glass after a few seconds of watching Collins and Tiffany hold on to each other.

"Anything."

"You told me it was an accident."

"Yes, everything was a catastrophic misfortune of events."

Rebecca glanced up into the glass and looked directly into Robert's eyes. "Thank you." She left, Collins, Tiffany, and Jones again bringing up the rear, left with her.

Collins drove the four of them back to his house for drinks to celebrate the victory and mourn the loss of Jaime Mason.

"Come on," Tiffany said with a smile as they walked up the pathway to Collins door. "We won!"

"What did we win?" Rebecca asked. "My mother is gone."

"Yeah, but the man who did it is safely behind bars. He can never hurt anybody ever again." They walked through the front door.

"I don't believe he would." Rebecca stood in the living room entrance. "I think I'm going to let him go."

"You are planning to do what?" Collins asked, the smile disappearing so fast from his face.

"I'm going to petition the court for his release." Rebecca stood tall as Collins hovered over her.

"Why?" Tiffany jumped in beside her newly found uncle.

"I wouldn't expect you to understand." Rebecca turned to leave.

"Try me," Collins and Tiffany both said together.

"I believe it was an accident."

"Accident or not, your mother is dead." Tiffany spoke up.

"She was dying," Rebecca defended her decision.

"We are all dying!" Collins got louder. "From the day we are born, we start to die. It's just, we don't know when our death date is."

"Well, what good would it do to lock a man away in prison who happened to be at the wrong place at the wrong time?"

"He wasn't in the wrong place at the wrong time. Your mother was," Tiffany too was getting louder.

"I have been angry for a very long time." Rebecca didn't raise her voice to match the other two. "If none of this had happened, you two wouldn't have met each other. At least, I got to apologize for everything before she passed. I got some peace and I think she did, too. I feel like this all happened for a reason and this is what I'm supposed to do. This is what my mother would have wanted me to do." She walked out the door and never looked back.

She was heading back to the courtroom.

Robert was escorted back down the hallway and into his cell. He leaned on the bed and stared up at the cracked ceiling. It reminded him of his apartment and he started to laugh.

"What's so funny?" a guard walking by asked.

"I feel right at home." Robert continued laughing.

"Well you should," the guard rolled his eyes, "you're going to be here for a very long time." He marched back to his post.

Robert laughed until his sides hurt. He was screwed. Everything he didn't want to happen, happened.

There was light streaming in through the barred windows, a beacon of small hope in the gloomy cell. Robert closed his eyes and slept.

Chapter 17

"I love you so much," Lindsey said as she rested her back against the wooden swing while leaning into Robert.

"I love you too." He nestled her into his embrace.

The spring air was quiet and warm as always during this time of year.

"I can't believe it's been fifty years since we've gotten married." Lindsey brushed back a strand of gray hair dancing around her face with a little help from the wind.

"I can't believe I've loved you more each day for fifty years." Robert pushed back his hat, which covered his bald head. "We've had a good life, haven't we?"

"We've had a great life." Lindsey stared out into the empty yard. "I could stay right here forever, as long as I'm with you."

Robert kissed the top of her head as he had done many times on this very swing over the years. "I could, too," he whispered, looking out over the horizon.

The sun was starting to settle down, changing the color of the sky to a deep purple.

"Isn't it beautiful?" Lindsey stared out.

"It sure is." Robert looked from the horizon to his wife "It sure is."

"Do we have to leave?"

"I thought that's what you wanted."

"This is what I want." She held him tighter.

"Everyone is coming tomorrow to help us move—the kids, the grandkids, everyone. Everything is all packed." Robert glanced through the window at the pile of boxes ready to be loaded and shipped off.

"I know." A tear started to form in her eye. *"I'm just so happy right now."*

"I know, but it's for the best." Robert brushed her hair with his hands. *"It's closer to the kids and family, and it's time for us to let someone else build memories here."*

"I know. I'm ready to move on and not ready to let go."

"I know how you feel." Robert soothed her.

The sun had almost disappeared, ready to be replaced by the night sky.

"Let's stay out here for a little longer. Let's just sit right here for now."

"As long as you want," Robert assured her, *"as long as you want."*

Robert sat there with his wife long after the sun went down. Someone he loved more than anything in the world.

"I love you," Lindsey whispered.

"I love you, too," Robert said with such meaning. *"I love you, too."*

Robert woke to a small noise coming from outside his cell.

He heard the gates open at the end of the hall, meaning someone was coming this way, probably another guard coming to relieve the one patrolling this area.

"You have a visitor," a chubby corrections officer spoke through the steel bars at Robert.

"Who is it?"

"You mean your secretary didn't call and tell you who it was?" The guard laughed at his own joke. "Turn around and place your hands on your head."

Robert did as he was told.

"Come on," the uniformed man barked. "This way."

He guided Robert back through the same doors he had went through on his first visitation, except he was pushed off into the room on the left.

He sat and waited in silence. "What now?" he mumbled to the empty room.

Robert gasped. "What's going on?" He eyed the woman who had entered.

"Can we have some time alone?" she asked the guard who had brought her.

He looked at her. "Holler if you need something."

Robert couldn't believe his eyes.

"Hello again." Rebecca stood there gazing through the Plexiglas at the man in chains.

"What are you doing here?" Robert asked, surprised. He had just talked to her. *What more could she want*, he wondered.

Rebecca didn't answer.

There was a brief silence.

"What are you doing here?" Robert repeated, his hands resting on the counter.

"I've come," she hesitated. "I've thought long and hard about this, maybe I should think longer, but I need to do this now. A lot of people aren't going to like this, but," she took a deep breath and exhaled slowly, "I'm petitioning the court for your release. I've already filed the motions and gave a statement as to why I think your case should be completely dropped. It's a long shot at best, but a lot of the paperwork hasn't been filed, which should make it easier and technically you haven't been sentenced yet. It's no longer up to me, but the court system as to whether my statement will be heard and receptive to the judge and the district attorney's office. Since everything is recent and still in the process of later proceedings, you may have an answer by the end of the week."

"What?" Robert jumped back, "Why?"

"I believe you." She spoke up with more confidence. "I was with you that night. I didn't see a man capable of murder. I believe what happened was truly an accident."

"I was drinking, maybe if I hadn't." Robert couldn't believe what he was hearing.

"I'm the one who forced you to come with me, maybe if I hadn't, you would have gone home sooner and nothing would have happened either. I'm just as responsible as you." She leaned against the glass separating her from her mother's killer.

"This doesn't explain why you are helping me?" Robert questioned, his heart pounding harder.

"My mother, I didn't know her very well." She took a deep breath. "I've talked to Tiffany, who spent more time with her than I did up until she passed away. She was dying, her heart was failing, she wouldn't have been around much longer and she would have suffered until the end. Tiffany said she was holding on as long as she did to see me." She lowered her head in pain. "My mother didn't have a lot of time on this earth. Apparently, God had bigger and better plans for her. I too know what it feels like to lose time. I lost it with her." She wiped her eyes with the end of her sleeve. "I know what happened was an accident, I can feel it in my heart. I know she wouldn't have wanted you to spend your life wasting away in prison, loosing what precious time we have here on Earth. You having to sit here and relive what happened every day."

Robert started to cry, too.

"I can feel how sorry you are, how it truly was an accident." Rebecca breathed softly again. "I don't know what the court will decide, but I'm letting you go." She backed off the divider.

Robert didn't say anything, he just wept like a baby. "I don't know what to say." He looked up to see Rebecca's white blouse disappear behind the door and away from view.

"I can't believe she's just letting him walk," Collins looked at Tiffany. Jones had left to go home to his wife.

"I know," Tiffany agreed as she sipped on the drink in her hand. "Maybe she's right, though."

"What?" Collins couldn't believe what he was hearing.

"Think about it for a second." Tiffany put her cup on the coffee table. "If Robert had never been in that accident, then like Rebecca said, we never would have met each other because you never would have been assigned to the case."

Collins looked at her with a grim expression.

"If you had never been assigned to the case, I never would have met you, and we wouldn't have each other—a family. Jaime Mason was already dying. I'm not saying that was the way to go, but her death brought us together. Maybe she would have wanted it this way."

"What? Lying on the street, waiting for help, or the part where she was in pain at the hospital up until her death?" Collins lifted himself up to walk the room and to relieve some anger.

"I was with her before everything went chaotic, before the incident. She was already in pain. She was holding on in hopes of seeing her daughter one more time. I was just like you when I heard what Rebecca said, but now I've thought about it. It makes sense."

"Listen to yourself." Collins turned. "How can you say that!"

"Just think about it."

Collins returned to his seat. *Could she be right*, he wondered as he leaned back into the cushion. The thought of his parent's accident lingered in his mind. "I don't like it," he grunted.

"I don't like what happened either, but it's her choice." Tiffany got up and came to sit with her uncle.

"Well, you're right about one thing." He turned to look at her. "It did bring you and me together, and you can stay as long as you'd like."

She smiled up at him.

ONE WEEK LATER

I can't believe it, Robert thought as he was being dismissed from prison. He got his clothes, wallet, and possessions back from when he was admitted. He walked outside onto the curb. "I can't believe it. Praise the Lord!" he shouted, arms held up high.

He waited for the taxi that was called to the prison to take him where he wanted to go. *There's just one more thing that I have to do.*

Robert pulled up to the countryside home for his last visit. "Wait here," he motioned to the taxi driver. "I'll be about ten minutes." Robert walked the familiar path and up the broken step, which he skipped, to the porch and through the broken down door. He made his way to the kitchen.

"Come on, come on." Robert searched through the cabinet doors. "There's gotta be a piece of paper somewhere."

He found a couple of wrinkled sheets in the cabinet above the stove. "Where's a pen?" He pulled out every drawer and found one at the back of one. "Here we go."

He walked over to the table and began to write.

Dear Lindsey,

I want to tell you how sorry I am for everything I did to you. You deserve so much better than anything I could ever give you. I'm sorry for the pain and every tear I ever made you cry. I was ready to start over. I guess I didn't have the courage to begin the journey. I know you hate me. I hate me, but in time I hope you will be able to forgive me. I hope you know I love you. I've always loved you and always will.

Please forgive me,
    Robert

Robert folded up the note and stuck it on the kitchen counter. Then he pulled out another wrinkled sheet of paper and wrote one more letter, knowing if this letter got delivered and was accepted, the first one would find its way to her. He stuck the one in his pocket and walked out the back door. The Envoy he had parked behind the house was gone, which he had expected. He glanced up at the bedroom as he walked around, the one he had come out here so many times to work on.

I guess there's another thing I will never be able to fix. He sighed as he walked toward the idle taxi and hopped in.

"Where to?"

"The police station," Robert replied.

The taxi man took off once again.

Collins walked up the station's step. "Time to get back to work," he mumbled as he walked through the doors.

"Detective Collins," the woman at the information desk said.

"Yes?"

"There's a note for you." She held out a neatly folded, wrinkled sheet of paper.

"Who's it from?" he asked, taking it from her.

"The man who brought it didn't leave a name, just asked if I would give it to you."

"Thanks," he mumbled and walked off toward his desk. He opened up the letter with his name on it.

Detective Collins,

I want you to know that I am truly sorry for everything that happened in the last week. For everything I put you through when you were chasing me. I wanted to let you know part of the reason I convicted myself of being guilty in court was due to the story you told me about your parents. I can't imagine how rough that must have been for you, along with losing your brother. I am glad you were able to find Tiffany and hope, along with finding her, you also find a part of yourself. I left the deed to the house in the country at my office. I want you to have it. I hope maybe you can find peace and comfort there.

Forgive me,

Robert Armes

"Sir?" Jones looked up from his desk. "Sir, are you OK?"

Collins folded the piece of paper up slowly and stuck it in his bottom desk drawer, along with the pictures he held close to his heart. "I'm fine." Collins wiped a tear from his eye. "Get back to work," he barked.

He picked up the phone and dialed his own home. "Tiffany, Tiffany, I understand what you and Rebecca have come to realize."

"That's great," came her voice on the other end.

"We are moving to your dad's and my old house." Collins smiled into the phone. "Pack your things. You and me are finally going home."

Robert stood outside the bus stop, forty dollars was all he had in his pocket after visiting the ATM. He didn't bother grabbing any clothes or items from the old house. He didn't bother stopping at his old apartment to pick up anything. The landlord would move in and take everything once he noticed Robert was gone, or had stopped paying rent.

It was best for him to start over, a new life with a clean slate. The bus pulled up at the corner and the doors opened with a swoosh. Robert climbed up the steps, skipping the second one from force of habit. He made his way toward the back and sat down next to the window.

He pressed his face up against the cold glass and watched the scenery fly by as the bus started to move away, leaving everything behind him.

Made in the USA
Charleston, SC
11 July 2013